Holding

Holding

Lorna Schultz Nicholson

James Lorimer & Company Ltd., Publishers
Toronto

James Lorimer & Company Ltd. acknowledges the support of the Ontario Arts Council. We acknowledge the support of the Government of Canada through the Book Publishing Industry Development Program (BPIDP) for our publishing activities. We acknowledge the support of the Canada Council for the Arts for our publishing program. We acknowledge the support of the Government of Ontario through the Ontario Media Development Corporation's Ontario Book Initiative.

Cover illustration: Greg Ruhl

Library and Archives Canada Cataloguing in Publication

Schultz Nicholson, Lorna

Holding / Lorna Schultz Nicholson.

(Sports Stories)

ISBN 978-1-55277-012-2 (bound)

ISBN 978-1-55277-011-5 (pbk.)

I. Title. II. Series: Sports stories (Toronto, Ont.)

PS8637.C58H64 2008 jC813'.6 C2007-907513-4

James Lorimer & Co. Ltd., Publishers
317 Adelaide Street West, Suite 1002
Toronto, Ontario
M5V 1P9
www.lorimer.ca

Distributed in the United States by:
Orca Book Publishers
P.O. Box 468
Custer, WA USA
98240-0468

Printed and bound in Canada.

CONTENTS

To my husband, Bob.
You're the best!

Acknowledgements

There is a real hockey school called the Okanagan Hockey School that runs all summer long in Penticton, British Columbia. Over the years that I have been writing my hockey books, the owners of this hockey school, Andy Oakes and Alan Kerr, have been so supportive. I'd like to thank them for allowing me to set up my table on registration day to sell my books, and for giving out my books as prizes to players at their hockey school.

I had a lot of fun writing this book! Writing and publishing a book takes a team of people. I would like to thank the Lorimer team, and especially my new editor, Faye Smailes. She was super encouraging and I know she's a big fan of *Holding*. As I hope you are! No one deserves more thanks than you, my readers. This is the last book in the series but don't worry, I'll have another series started soon! So stay tuned.

1 Introductions

Josh Watson walked into the school classroom and grinned. This was how every classroom, all year, should look. As summer home to the Okanagan Hockey School camp, the classroom had been made into a dorm room and already looked messy. Most of the cots were taken. Blankets, sleeping bags, and pillows were thrown haphazardly on the makeshift beds.

Josh flung his bedding on an empty cot and shoved his suitcase underneath. He hadn't bothered to bring much with him from Calgary to this camp in Penticton. The most important stuff, his hockey equipment, was already across the street in an equipment room. He wiped the sweat off his brow. It had to be forty degrees outside.

He crashed into the wall as he was bumped from behind. His cousin Troy Watson pushed past Josh, carrying an enormous bag stuffed to bursting.

"Man, it's hot," said Troy. "But not a bug in sight."

Josh laughed. Troy was from Winnipeg, Manitoba, home of the mosquito. "This is going to be a blast, the two of us playing hockey together in the summer," Josh said. He really hoped that would be true. He grinned nervously at Troy. "Usually we're just hanging by your pool."

"I'm pumped," said Troy. "I hope your friends are as good as you say."

"Let's set up our beds, then try to find everyone." Josh still couldn't believc that he would be playing on a team with so many of his old friends and teammates. When Josh and his old friend Sam Douglas had decided to attend the camp, they had tried to get friends to join up so they would have a stacked team. Josh could tell who had already arrived by the different sports bags lying around the room. Josh spotted the Kanata Kings' bags that belonged to Sam and his friend Steven Becker. On the other side of the room, Peter Kuiksak's Edmonton Arrows' bag sat under a messy cot. Tony Seeley and Nick Bell had come in from Calgary like Josh, but there was no sign of their stuff yet. Josh knew the bag with the Kelowna Stars patch belonged to Kevin Jennings.

"Watson! When did you get here?" Sam ran in the room, followed by Peter.

"Douglas! Kuiksak!" Josh high-fived Sam. Peter slapped his hand too, the force almost knocking Josh to the ground.

Josh spun around and tackled Sam, trying to push him onto a cot. He could tell right away that his goalie friend had bulked up since Josh had seen him last spring. When Josh tried to get Sam in a headlock, he realized Sam had grown taller too. In a surprise twist, Sam headlocked Josh and they both fell onto one of the cots. The springs creaked, then the cot bounced up, tossing a sleeping bag into the air.

"They're not the best beds in the world," said Josh, laughing.

"You got that right," said Troy. "The mattresses are about a centimetre thick. My bed at home is one of those real thick ones."

Josh glanced at Troy. When they were together, Josh was used to ignoring his cousin's bragging. But he hadn't thought that Troy would act like that when he was with a bunch of guys he'd never met before. Sam got up and stuck out his hand. "Hi, I'm Sam. You must be Josh's cousin."

"Yeah. I'm Troy." Troy spoke with confidence. Josh wished he could be more like that when he met new people.

"Yo!" Kevin Jennings sauntered into the room, wearing aviator shades. Judging by his dark tan, he'd obviously spent July on the beach.

"Hey, look. It's poster boy," said Sam.

"Yeah, well, I can't help it if I'm a chick magnet."

"What did you do to your hair?" Josh asked,

laughing. Kevin's long brown hair was now hockey tape white.

"What can I say? Girls love blondes."

Steven Becker barrelled into the room with Tony on his heels.

After a round of back-slapping and introductions, Josh asked, "Did you guys get your jerseys?"

"They're awesome," said Sam.

Josh held up one of the black jerseys. Printed on the back was the name they had chosen for their team — *NHL Selects*.

Sam grinned. "This name suits us, seeing as we're all playing in the NHL one day."

"You think?" Peter shoved his hands in his pockets.

"Dude, you're the one who's going to go first-round in the Bantam draft next year," said Steven.

Peter shrugged. "It's a long way to the pros."

Sam ignored Peter's modesty. "I met another guy on our team," said Sam. "He's big, which is awesome. We need size."

"Hell-o," said Steven. "Just because you're a shrimp doesn't mean everyone is."

"I'm not a shrimp anymore. I'm catching up to you." Sam flexed his arms. "Look at these babies."

Josh flexed too. "My pipes are massive." Josh's scrawny arms stuck out the side of his body like tree twigs.

"Yeah, right, Wattie," said Sam. "Your freckles are bigger than your arms."

"I don't think you've put on a pound since last summer," said Troy. He flexed and his biceps bulged. Josh tried to stand tall. It seemed everyone was growing but Josh and Tony.

Josh pulled a crumpled schedule out of the pocket of his shorts. "I can't wait to get on the ice. We have power skating tonight."

"I hate power skating," replied Troy.

Troy pulled out a compact sound system. Josh recognized it as one of the latest and greatest. "Look what I brought for the dressing room. It has rad sound." Troy docked his iPod into it, and rap music blared from the speakers.

Next, Troy pulled out a portable DVD player. "I got this before I left," he said. "It's got twelve playing hours." He pulled out a DVD case. "I brought tons of movies."

"Sweet," said Sam.

"Yeah, sweet," said Peter, obviously impressed.

As Troy got out his boxed set of cards and chips for Texas Hold'em poker, all the guys gathered around. Josh had already seen all of Troy's new stuff, so he opened his backpack and pulled out three books.

"You brought books?" Troy's voice sounded over the loud music. "That's lame. It's summer vacation."

"Yeah, and in summer I get to read what I want." Josh picked up a book titled *Bone*. "This is a really cool graphic novel. And I read *Lord of the Rings* every summer." He tossed a beat-up copy of *The Two Towers* on his bed. It was followed by a book with *The Thief Lord* in silver print on the cover. "I just started this, and it's awesome."

"Hey, I read that," said Steven. "It's about Venice, Italy. I liked it."

"Yo, bros," said Kevin. "Why are we talking about books when we should be talking about girls? This place is filled with hot babes."

"Girls?" asked Josh. "We don't have any girls on our team."

"Yeah, but there's a couple on the other teams. And the cafeteria is loaded with them! They're working right now," said Kevin. "I hope the hot ones serve us our food."

"I saw some girls working at the concession too," said Peter.

"Have you guys already done the concession thing?" Josh looked at Sam and Peter.

"Yeah," said Sam. "But we'll walk back with you."

"What kind of stuff do they have?" Josh didn't like to make a big deal of it, but he needed to know where he could get food to help keep his diabetes regulated. Over the past few years, he'd learned to keep it under control by playing it safe. Josh worked hard to control his diabetes so he could play high-level hockey and attend overnight hockey camps.

"The usual," said Sam. "Candy, chips, hot dogs, pizza."

"I already had pizza," said Peter. "It was awesome."

"It looked disgusting." Sam grimaced.

Troy pulled a wad of bills from the pocket of his board shorts. "How much money are you putting in concession, Josh?"

"A hundred."

"That's it?" Troy looked at Josh, his brows squished together. "My parents gave me three hundred."

"Three hundred?" Sam's eyes widened. "Lucky you. You're loaded."

★ ★ ★

"NHL Selects, over here!"

Josh glanced at a dark-haired guy holding up a sign with *NHL Selects* printed on it in big red letters. He was so tall that the sign almost reached the branches of the trees.

"There's our counsellor," said Josh.

"I heard he plays for the Vancouver Giants," said Sam. "He's their best forward."

"They won the Memorial Cup last year." Josh joined the rest of the guys gathering in a half-circle around their camp counsellor.

"My name is Gerald Wilfur," he said, "and I'm your counsellor for the next two weeks. There are some rules you need to follow." He stopped for a moment to scan the group. "We're missing a few players."

Gerald cupped his hands around his mouth. "NHL Selects," he yelled. "Meet here!"

Over the next few minutes, teams slowly came together out of the masses of kids milling around. To fill out the NHL Selects, Josh and his friends were joined by three players from Alaska. Cameron seemed to do all the talking for the Alaskan group. Bryce was the smallest and really funny, and Zack, a goalie, had long bangs that hid how his face was marked with zits. A couple of huge guys from Saskatoon, Barry and Carl, rounded out the team.

Gerald launched into his rules spiel: lights-out at nine-thirty; zero tolerance for bullying, drinking, drugs, and gambling.

Once the rules were covered, the team armed themselves with sticks and balls and headed out to the black tarmac of the school playground for ball hockey.

"I'm on the skins side," Kevin whipped his T-shirt over his head. "It's too hot to be a shirt."

Josh hadn't been out in the sun much through the summer. It sucked being a redhead. "I'll play shirts," he yelled.

Within a few minutes the teams were decided. Troy had spoken up quickly to make sure he was on Barry and Carl's team opposite Josh. They were playing no-goalies, so you had to hit the post to get a goal.

They tossed to see who had possession first, and Josh's team won. Peter stick-handled the ball as he ran up the wing. Josh took off too. Peter passed to him. Spotting Sam on the other wing, Josh sent the ball over. Sam cradled the ball on his stick and ran a few strides, then wound up for a slapshot. Troy ducked in and picked off the ball before Sam got his shot off. Josh put on the brakes and changed directions. Full speed, Troy ran toward Josh's net. Josh tried to angle him off the ball, but Troy stayed solid.

"Shoot," yelled Carl.

Troy wound up and his shot just missed the post. Carl picked up the rebound, but Peter was on him right away. They jostled for possession. Through sheer determination, Peter managed to get the ball going the other way. Josh ran to pick it up, but Carl had already come back. Relentlessly, he tried to lift Josh's stick. Josh held tight and pushed him. The guy was a tank.

Carl kept at him, but Josh wouldn't back down. Josh saw Sam coming in to support him and he batted the ball over to him. Troy scooped in and rifled the ball down the tarmac toward their net. The ball bounced out of bounds.

"I'm not getting it," said Troy.

"You shot it out," said Sam.

Everyone took a moment to wipe the sweat from their faces before Peter said, "I'll get it."

The play went back and forth. Josh ran up and down, and the sweat cruised down his face, soaking the front of his T-shirt.

Josh and his team were losing 11–8 when Barry stopped playing.

"It's like a sauna out here," he said. "I'm going back to the room." He picked up his shirt from the ground and tossed it on top of his head.

"I'm right behind you," said Carl.

"I think I'll quit too," said Troy. Just like Barry, he picked up his shirt and put it on his head. "Anyone want to watch a movie?"

Josh shrugged. "I'll keep playing." He could watch a movie anytime.

"Yeah, me too," said Peter.

"I'm in," said Sam.

Josh and the remaining guys played until it was time for dinner.

2 Starting Small

The cafeteria was in the arena. Local girls were working, serving food to the players.

"That blond is so hot," whispered Kevin. He stared at the girl as he wound his spaghetti around his fork.

"Whoa." Sam pointed to the wad of pasta on the end of Kevin's fork. It was as big as a baseball. Josh nudged Sam and they laughed.

"Bet you can't shove that in your mouth," said Troy.

"Bet you I can," said Kevin.

"Five bucks," said Troy.

"You're on." Kevin opened his mouth wide and shoved the spaghetti in. His cheeks bulged and he looked as if he had balloons stuffed in them. Josh thought for sure he would have to spit out the spaghetti, but Kevin continued to chew.

Josh laughed so hard he had to bang his fists on the table to get control. All the other guys were howling with laughter as well.

As Kevin's jaw worked at the huge mouthful of food, Troy stood up and pulled a five-dollar bill out of his pocket and threw it on the table.

Kevin pocketed the money. Then he made a big deal about wiping his mouth. "Hey, thanks, man. When we bet, usually no one comes through with the cashola. Good on yah." He held up his thumb.

"I always come through on a bet," said Troy, with attitude.

★ ★ ★

After dinner, Josh's team had a power skating session with no pucks. They shared the ice with Team Mexico.

"Listen up," said the power skating instructor. "First drill is stop-and-start. The cones are set up against the boards. Skate to each cone, stop, then go to the next cone. Zigzag down the ice. It doesn't do any good if you cheat yourself by stopping only on one side. Stop one side, then the next. Okay, I want everyone lined up at the end."

Although Josh skated hard to get to the end zone and be first in line, he didn't quite make it and ended up in the middle. Peter managed to be third in the lineup, right behind Carl and Barry. Some players from Team Mexico were clumped in the middle with Josh.

When the whistle blew to start the drill, Josh couldn't help but notice that Carl and Barry were explosive skaters. They raced toward the first cone. Peter followed on their heels and Troy went after Peter. Troy had always been a better player than Josh, even before his growth spurt. Josh tried not to be jealous, but sometimes he wanted to be the guy who ruled.

Josh sucked in a deep breath, waiting his turn. A couple of the players from Team Mexico looked pretty good. When it was finally Josh's time to go, he got down low and took off. He accelerated past two guys and almost managed to catch two more. When he hit the end, he bent over to catch his breath. His heart was beating like crazy. His head was buzzing. He looked up to see Sam and the other three goalies barrelling down the ice.

After they did the stop-and-start drill four more times, the power skating instructor blew his whistle and split up the teams. The NHL Selects were together at one end.

"We have some good players on our team," Peter said to Josh.

"Yeah, I'm glad I'm with the guys from Saskatoon and not against them."

"Me too," said Peter. "And your cousin's good."

"He was top scorer on his Bantam Triple-A team."

"You know, you've really improved since last summer," said Peter.

"Thanks." Josh straightened his shoulders. Peter's vote of confidence meant a lot to Josh. Peter was one of the best Bantam players in Alberta.

At the blue line, the instructor pointed to the cones set up on half of the ice. "Skate to the cone and, when you hit it, pivot and skate backward to the next cone. Work on your transitions." The instructor blew his whistle and all the players raced to the end zone.

Josh ended up in the middle again. Troy somehow had nudged his way to third in line. Peter was fourth. Tony was behind Josh.

"By the looks of it," whispered Tony in his squeaky voice, "we're going to be able to kick Team Mexico's butt."

"I hope we win the entire tournament," said Josh.

By the end of the power skating session, Josh's legs felt like wet sand. Skating without pucks was always a killer.

Gerald met them all outside the arena. "Put your equipment away and take a shower. Remember, lights-out at nine-thirty. You have a busy day tomorrow."

"Nine-thirty," said Troy to Josh under his breath. "I don't think so. I never go to bed at nine-thirty, not even during the school year. I'm going to organize a card game."

Josh had no desire to play cards. When he got back to the room, he sat around with Sam and Peter and they talked, catching up on hockey talk and what they had done so far with the summer. Sam had picked strawberries to make some extra money, and

Peter had gone home to the North to see his family. Josh had a job helping his dad one day a week in his office.

Ten minutes before lights-out, Josh headed to the bathroom. Because of his diabetes, he liked leaving himself a little more time than the other guys to get ready for bed. He had just finished pricking his finger to check his blood sugar when Troy walked in, carrying a towel, his toothbrush, and toothpaste.

"I can't believe what you have to do before you go to bed," he said.

"It's no big deal." Josh was used to it. He had to check his blood sugar and record it in a little book. If it was high, he had to give himself a shot of insulin; if it was low, he needed to eat something sweet.

"I hope you don't get sick partway through camp and have to go home early, or start playing lousy."

"I'm not going to get sick. I've told you a million times, my diabetes doesn't make any difference in how I play."

"Yeah, my mom said that too. But, still, you have to give yourself needles."

"There are lots of athletes who have diabetes." Josh had learned that some people thought his diabetes would keep him from being a serious athlete, but he never thought that Troy would be so immature about it.

Troy squeezed his tube of toothpaste. "I can't wait

to play tomorrow. I hope I'm on a line with Carl and Barry. Those guys are amazing."

"Peter is good too."

"I hope our coach stacks some lines." Troy rinsed his mouth, then looked at himself in the mirror. "And has power play and penalty kill lines."

"We meet our coach tomorrow at game time." Josh put his kit away and took out his toothbrush.

"Yeah, after a ton of dry-land," muttered Troy.

"I like dry-land."

Troy rolled his eyes at Josh then gave him a lop-sided grin. "You would. You like power skating too." He playfully pushed him.

Josh ignored the push. "All the pros do dry-land," he said.

"Yeah, but we're not pros, bro."

Sam roared into the bathroom, sliding across the tiled floor in his flip-flops. Steven was right behind him. "Gerald just gave us thirty extra minutes before lights-out," said Sam.

"Wow, a whole thirty minutes," said Troy sarcastically. "That will only take us to ten — and we're on summer holidays."

"Let's watch a movie," said Josh.

"I'm playing more cards," said Troy.

Once the DVD player was set up, Josh sat on the floor to watch with the guys from Alaska, and Sam, Peter, Tony, and Nick.

Troy, Carl, Barry, and Kevin were sitting cross-legged on the floor, playing Texas Hold-em. Troy was winning and had a pile of chips in front of him. After a few rounds, Kevin threw his cards in the middle and said, "I'm out."

"That's it for everyone," said Gerald from his cot. He was lying on his back reading the latest issue of *Hockey Now*. He put down his paper and went to the light switch. "You've got thirty seconds to get the card game cleaned up and the DVD player off." He started counting backwards.

"Come on," said Troy. "I'm winning."

"Yeah, and if you don't get some sleep you won't win your hockey game tomorrow."

"And we want to win," said Carl. He threw in his cards. Barry threw in his cards too.

Once everything was cleaned up and everyone was on their beds, Gerald flicked off the light. Josh lay on his back and closed his eyes. He could hear everyone breathing. He wondered how he was going to sleep with sixteen people breathing at different times, making noises that sounded like an elementary school band warming up. At home he had his own room.

Suddenly, a huge fart ripped through the room.

"Gross!" Sam yelled. "Steven, was that you?"

"No!"

"Who was it, then?"

"Quiet, guys," said Gerald. "And can the gas. This

room doesn't need any extra heat."

"It was Josh!" yelled Troy.

At the sound of his name, Josh piped up. "It wasn't me!"

Tony started laughing and waving his sleeping bag at Josh, as if he was trying to get rid of the smell.

"I said, it wasn't me!" But Josh was laughing too.

"Quiet!" yelled Gerald.

The quiet lasted for a few seconds. Then it was punctuated by Barry's low voice. "Let's tell stories like we're around a campfire," he said. "I've got one. My brother just graduated from high school in Saskatoon and is going to play for an AHL team next year."

"Dude, that's not a campfire story," said Sam.

"If we're telling *real stories,*" said Troy, "then my dad owns a big software company and is about to sign a multi-million dollar deal."

Josh groaned. Why did Troy have to brag?

"And once upon a time I had two stupid brothers." Sam used a deep, scary voice as if he was telling a ghost story.

Everyone started laughing. "You are so not making me shake with fear, dude," said Barry.

"I'm from Alaska and it's cold in the winter," said Cameron.

"Duh, as if we didn't know that," retorted Kevin.

"Well, I bet you didn't know that, per capita, Alaska consumes the most ice cream in the United

States, and that more than half of the world's glaciers are in Alaska."

"Are the glaciers made of ice cream?" Sam asked. Everyone started howling.

"Guys, it's time to quiet down," interrupted Gerald.

"Hey counsellor-man, tell us about winning the Memorial Cup," said Barry.

"Okay. But only if you guys promise to go to sleep afterward."

"We promise!" they all yelled. The vote in the room was unanimous.

"We were down by two going into the second." At the sound of Gerald's voice, everyone quieted. Josh wanted to hear every word he had to say.

Gerald continued, "We went to the dressing room, and our coach gave it to us. He kicked a garbage can and told us to believe in ourselves, and then left. We were totally fired up. I was captain, so I had to talk to the guys. We talked for the rest of the clean, then we went out and scored two goals in twenty seconds. It was an amazing feeling to hold the trophy and skate around the ice."

"Can you imagine winning the Stanley Cup?" asked Carl.

"That would be the ultimate," said Gerald.

"It would be so unbelievable," said Josh.

"Winning a trophy like that takes a lot of hard

work. And sleep," Gerald said. "It's time to hit the hay so you can win this tournament. Start small, guys, and work your way up. Now go to sleep."

After four more farts from the corners of the room, Josh had fallen asleep.

3 First Game

"Time to get up, guys!"

Josh opened one eye to see Gerald, already dressed in his counsellor's track suit, standing at the door of the dorm room. Josh stretched to get the kinks out of his body. His sleep had been awful.

"Breakfast is in fifteen minutes," said Gerald.

Most of the guys groaned, but Troy groaned the loudest. "I haven't been up before eleven all summer. These beds are brutal."

"Just wait," said Gerald, "until you have the six a.m. ice time. Then I'll be getting you up at five-thirty."

"No way," said Troy.

"Yes way," shot back Gerald. "I'll see you guys at breakfast."

Excited about the game later that night, Josh thought the morning might drag, but he was happy to find that it sped by. First was dry-land plyometrics, then they took a trip to the gym. Carl and Barry were by far the strongest guys on the team when it came to lifting. Troy came in a close third.

In the afternoon there was a motivational seminar. Some of the guys complained about going to the lecture, saying they wanted to sleep instead, but Gerald herded them over to the hall anyway.

"Why do we have to do dumb stuff like go to *talks?*" said Troy.

"I bet this is going to be so-o-o boring," said Carl.

"Hey," said Troy, pointing to Gerald, who was walking ahead with the players from Alaska. Troy jerked his head toward the dorm. "Anyone up for ditching this and playing some cards?"

"Not me," said Josh.

"Me either," said Peter.

Carl glanced at Troy, then looked ahead at Gerald's back, which was moving away from the dawdling boys.

"He won't notice," whispered Troy. "Come on."

"Okay," said Carl, grinning. "You're on." He turned to Barry. "You in too?"

Barry's grin was like a mirror image of Carl's. "You bet. But we have to make it look as if we're going into the building."

Troy slapped Josh on the back. "If Gerald asks, say we had to go to the can."

Josh nodded but kept walking. Peter walked up beside him.

"I wouldn't lie for him," said Peter.

Sam hustled to walk on Josh's other side. "I wouldn't either," said Sam.

Josh didn't say anything. He hoped that it wouldn't come to that.

The motivational session was anything but boring. Josh enjoyed getting out of the sun and into a cool, darkened room. Instead of a lecture, the motivational speaker told them great stories and gave tips to help them stay focused and inspired. One tip stuck out to Josh in particular.

"Holding onto anger off the ice is like holding onto a hot coal with the intent of throwing it at someone else," the speaker said. "You're the one who gets burned."

The speaker stood up and stepped closer to the guys. "Now, just before we end, I'll tell one last joke."

"This guy's got the best jokes," whispered Sam.

"Wayne Gretzky, Mario Lemieux, and Steve Yzerman all die and meet in heaven. God, sitting in his chair, turns to Lemieux and says, 'Mario, what do you believe in?' 'I believe hockey is the greatest thing in the world and the best sport in history.' To that God says, 'Take the seat to my left. And Steve, what do you believe in?' 'I believe bravery is the best.' To that God says, 'Take the seat to my right. And Wayne, what do you believe in?' 'I believe you're sitting in my seat.'"

The audience burst into laughter.

The motivational speaker held up his hands and

the room quieted immediately. "We're going to finish with some visualization. I want you to close your eyes and concentrate on seeing yourself playing the way you want to play."

The room stilled. Josh closed his eyes and tried to block out any external sounds. He tried to see himself shooting really hard and body-checking like a big guy. He repeated the images in his mind, making them sharper and more real each time.

Finally, they were told to open their eyes. Sam looked at Josh and said, "That was so amazing. I stopped a million pucks."

"Yeah, and I hit the biggest guy and didn't fall down," said Josh.

Josh and Sam met up with Peter, Steven, Kevin, and Tony outside the hall. They were all walking back to the room when Sam said, "Uh-oh. Here comes Gerald and he looks totally confused."

"Have you guys seen Troy, Carl, and Barry?" Gerald asked.

"Nope," said Sam.

Steven and Kevin echoed Sam. Peter just shrugged. Tony didn't say anything.

"Were they in the session?" Gerald asked.

Josh thought fast. "I saw them walking into the building, but we didn't sit with them."

"Okay. As long as they attended. My job is to get you guys to every session."

That was close, thought Josh. He hadn't exactly lied to Gerald, but for some reason Josh still felt guilty.

Barry, Carl, and Troy had cleaned up the card game by the time the others got back to the room. Troy greeted Josh with a big grin and a high-five, but Barry and Carl were strangely quiet. Josh was surprised, as the two big guys from Saskatoon usually seemed to be anything but the silent type.

★ ★ ★

As the first game of the tournament got closer, Josh could see that the motivational session was really well-timed. He felt himself getting geared up to hit the ice and finally meet the coach for the NHL Selects.

"Who's our coach?" Steven asked Gerald.

"Manny Smith," replied Gerald. "You guys are lucky. He's an assistant coach with the Vancouver Canucks."

"They were in the Stanley Cup finals last year," said Josh. "Naslund says he's the best coach he ever had, and Naslund is so good right now."

Gerald puffed out his chest and flexed his biceps. "And I'll be your assistant coach, so that's true luck."

Then Steven flexed his biceps. "I'm bigger than you, man."

Gerald nodded. "You probably are. Now, let's get going."

"We're going to kick some butt!" said Kevin.

"Save your big talk for the ice. That's where it counts." Gerald moved toward the door.

Josh picked up his jersey and flung it over his shoulder. He was ready to play hockey.

When Manny Smith walked into the dressing room, all the guys cheered. It was one thing to see him on TV — behind the bench, dressed in a suit — but to see him in person was amazing. Josh couldn't help notice that the coach looked fit in his Okanagan track suit, even though he had some grey hair like Josh's dad. Coach Smith held up his hand. "Hey, guys. My name is Manny, and I'm your coach for the next two weeks.

"The purpose of this camp," he started in right away, "is for you to get the most out of every single session. The camp is designed to make sure you are taught every aspect of being an athlete; a hockey player.

"But," continued Manny, "because there's nothing like actual play, in this camp you also compete against other teams in a real tournament."

All the guys cheered. Josh made sure he was loud. Manny smiled and let everyone hoot and holler for a few seconds before he held up his hand.

"Okay, okay. This is a tournament that we may win, or we may not. But if you give your all, every shift of every game, then you'll become a better player. Your first game is against Team Mexico." He paused. "Team

Mexico comes up almost every year. They may not be the most skilled players, but they are hard, hard workers. If you give them an opportunity to steal the puck, they will, because they never give up." He looked around the room. "Now, I've looked over the team roster and set up some lines."

Manny read off the names. He kept the guys from Alaska together, and put Barry and Carl with Kevin. Josh noticed that Troy looked disappointed that his name wasn't called with the guys from Saskatoon.

"Josh — "

When he heard his name, Josh sat up tall.

" … Troy, and Peter," finished Manny.

Josh sucked in a deep breath. He was on a line with Peter! Josh glanced at Troy and held up his thumb. Troy didn't respond. *Whatever*, thought Josh.

"Ice is ready," said Gerald.

As they all stood and headed out, Josh tried to shake off how annoyed he was with Troy. Who cared what Troy thought? Josh got to play with Peter, who was better than Troy anyway.

During warm-up, Josh tried to make his shots on Sam as hard as the shots he had visualized that afternoon. Sam was in net for this first game. The two team goalies would rotate games and, if the team made it to the final, they would split the game to make it fair.

Josh, Troy, and Peter were on the bench when the puck dropped. Carl and Barry picked up the puck and flew toward Team Mexico's net. They were obviously the fastest skaters on the ice. They passed back and forth, but didn't give one pass to Kevin, who pounded his stick on the ice to let them know he was open.

In a skilled move, Barry picked up a pass from Carl and blasted it into the net.

"Man, they're good," said Troy. He turned to Josh. "Between the two of them they scored over 200 points in their Bantam league this year. They were a dominating force."

The whistle blew and Josh turned his attention back to the ice. Barry, Carl, and Kevin skated to the bench. Gerald opened the gate, and Josh skated to his position on right wing. The play was in Team Mexico's end.

The ref dropped the puck. Troy at centre won the face-off and sent the puck back. Josh drove to the net, hoping for a rebound. On the point, Cameron fired off a shot, but it went wide. Josh hustled behind the net. He bumped the Mexican guy off the puck and looked up. Troy was wide open. Peter was in front tying up the defence. Josh fired a hard pass to Troy, who one-timed it. The puck sailed into the back of the net.

"Great shot," said Josh to Troy.

Josh thought that Troy might thank him for the pass. But all he did was skate to the red line to get ready for the face-off, and look to the bench for acknowledgement.

Peter skated up beside Josh. "Great pass," he said.

"Thanks. You tied up the guy so Troy could get the shot away."

"He rifled it pretty good."

They lined up and waited for the face-off. Again, Josh managed to get the puck on his stick and went wide, heading toward the net. Troy yelled that he was open. Peter, over on the other wing, was also open, but it was a longer pass to send it to Peter. Josh made a quick decision. Peter was good enough to pick up the pass and probably get a shot on net. If Josh drove to the net, he might have a chance to score on a rebound. The Mexican defence wasn't that strong, so Josh sailed the puck over to Peter.

It wasn't a perfect pass and Peter was stick-checked. There was a scramble and the puck bounced. Josh quickly skated in for support. He lifted the stick of one of the Mexican players and pushed the puck up the boards for Peter to grab. Peter looked up, saw Troy circling in his high slot position, and sniped him a pass. In a smooth move around the Mexican defence, Troy nailed a top-cheese shot. The goalie didn't have a chance.

After congratulating Troy, Josh skated back to the bench.

"Great support," said Coach Manny to Josh, tapping his helmet.

"That was a sizzling applesauce," said Josh to Peter, using hockey lingo for a great assist.

Peter nodded.

Troy leaned over and said to Josh, "Next time I'm in the clear, give me the pass. I was wide open."

"You were open because you cherry-pick in the slot," Josh responded. "You don't want to get banged around so you never come in for support or go to the boards."

"That's not true."

"Yes, it is." Josh steered his attention away from Troy and back to the ice just in time to watch the Alaska line score a goal.

The game ended with the NHL Selects beating Team Mexico 10–3.

Together, Barry and Carl had scored five of the goals. Troy had picked up two, and Peter had netted two as well. Cameron from the Alaska line had scored one from the point. Josh had picked up an assist, and he knew that an assist was as good as a goal. His team had played well. That's what really counted the most.

4 Up at Dawn

"Fifteen minutes, guys," announced Gerald. "Then it's lights out. If you're quiet tonight, then tomorrow we can do joke night."

"Joke night?" Sam bellowed.

"Yeah, joke night. But the jokes have to be clean."

"All right!" Josh high-fived Sam. Then he whispered to him, "I've got a good joke to play on Troy tomorrow morning."

Five-thirty a.m. came too early. Josh could barely open his eyes.

Half asleep, Josh brushed his teeth, then went back to the room. Troy still lay curled on his cot. "Hey, Sam," Josh whispered.

Sam tiptoed over, holding Barry's shaving cream and a string. He squirted shaving cream into Troy's open hand.

Josh took the string. "Troy," he called softly. He gently dangled the string on Troy's cheek.

"Yeah," Troy mumbled. He reached up to stop the tickling feeling. When he did, he smacked his face, smearing it with shaving cream.

"Time to get up!" yelled Josh.

Troy immediately sat up and ran his hand through his hair. Then he glanced at the white foam in his hand. "What the heck?"

"Time for practice!"

Josh and Sam ran from the room. "Next time," said Josh, panting, "we should draw on his face."

Outside, the sky was light and clear, with not a cloud in sight. By midday it would be a scorcher. Josh stared at the horizon line, at the burning red of the sun just peeking up. Gerald frowned, obviously deep in thought.

"Troy is on his way," said Josh to Gerald.

"Here he comes," Sam whispered.

With his hair sticking up, and some shaving cream still on his face, Troy looked like a ghost from a horror movie.

Barry and Carl laughed the loudest, and Josh overheard Barry whisper, "Serves him right."

Serves him right for what? Josh wondered. He had thought that Troy was tight with the guys from Saskatoon.

Today they were practicing at McLaren arena. Another team was already on the bus when the NHL Selects boarded, and most of them were slouched over the seats, their heads resting between their hands, trying to catch a few extra winks.

Josh found an empty seat and Troy flopped down beside him.

"I'll get you guys back," said Troy.

"You have to admit, it was a good trick."

"Yeah, it was good. But mine will be better." He grinned.

★ ★ ★

As soon as Josh stepped on the ice, he felt the refreshing and familiar jolt of cold arena air wake him up completely. Josh skated around the ice, stretching with his stick over his back to warm up. He lowered into a lunge to stretch out his legs.

When the whistle blew, both teams skated toward the coaches. Judging from the way the other team skated, they were good, a team to beat.

"What team are we on with?" Troy quietly asked Josh as they gathered in front of Coach Manny and the white board.

"Montana, I think."

Troy nodded. "They look decent."

The practice went a lot quicker than Josh anticipated because they were kept constantly moving. Josh liked the way Coach Manny didn't make them do the same drill over and over again, which could make practice boring. The hour and a half was up in no time.

On the way back to the dorm, Troy struck up a conversation with the guys from the Montana team. Josh just watched silently, wishing he could be like Troy and talk to everyone.

"Is your whole team from Montana?" Troy asked.

"Almost. There are a few guys from Canada on our team. And a few from England."

"England? I didn't know they played hockey." Troy paused for a second before he asked, "Where's your room?"

"I think we're beside you."

"Cool," said Troy.

Troy turned to look at Josh. "Who do we play tonight?"

"Grand Prairie." Josh had memorized the schedule with Sam the night before.

"I've heard they're a strong team," said the guy from Montana. "We lost to Switzerland last night. They're fast and skilled."

"Yeah, I've heard that," said Josh.

As he got up to leave, Troy turned to the Montana guys and said, "I'll come over later. I've got a great card game you'll love."

Josh wondered why Troy wanted to play cards with the Montana guys instead of with Barry and Carl again. True, while Josh was at camp with some of his best friends, Troy had to actually meet new guys and make friends. But why couldn't he try harder to make friends with the guys on their team? Anyway, there was so much more to do at camp than play cards. And winning a card game was nothing compared with winning a hockey game — or a whole tournament!

★ ★ ★

In the afternoon, the players had some down time. Josh went back to the room to read, but the heat of the afternoon put him to sleep. When he jolted awake, he felt a bit confused, until he realized that it was midday and he was at a summer hockey camp. He propped himself up on his elbow and his book tumbled to the floor. As he picked it up, he glanced around the room. Gerald was on his cot snoring, and the rest of his teammates were also asleep … except for Troy. His bed was empty. Where was the guy? Still playing cards?

5 Frustration

Josh walked to the concession between Sam and Troy. "The team we play tonight is supposed to be good," said Sam. "I wish I was going to be in goal."

"Yeah," replied Josh. "I can't wait to play. It'll be a tougher game than last night, more of a challenge."

"I don't care, as long as we win," said Troy.

"Let's get pizza," said Peter, nudging Josh from behind. When Josh laughed at his friend's never-ending appetite for pizza, Peter added, "They make good pizza here. Not like where I come from. You guys have good pepperoni. In Tuktoyaktuk they make it with caribou meat that's raw."

"That's disgusting," said Josh.

"You're such a liar, Peter," said Sam.

"Yeah, well, Josh believed me." Peter grinned.

"But Josh is gullible."

Josh ran into Sam, body-slamming him. "You don't even know what gullible means," laughed Josh.

Then they ran into the arena and up the stairs, arriving at the canteen breathless.

They all bought something except Troy. Instead, he asked if he could take some money out of his concession account. The workers didn't know what to do. He produced his ID and talked convincingly until the girl gave him fifty dollars.

"Man, you're smooth," said Sam. "I'm going to start calling you Slippery."

Troy wrestled with Sam, getting him in a half-nelson hold. Josh could see the intense look on Troy's face. Then he saw him tighten his grasp.

"Hey, let go!" Sam squirmed until he had freed himself. "Relax, man. It was just a joke."

Troy backed away, but Josh could tell that Sam wasn't impressed.

★ ★ ★

Josh lined up at the red line. Tonight his line was the first. The winger opposite Josh was huge. Josh leaned over, waiting for the puck to drop. As soon as it left the ref's hand he anticipated its direction. Troy took control and sent the puck back.

Josh sped to the boards, hoping his defence would fire it up to him. Sure enough, the puck bounced off the boards right by Josh. He picked it up and raced forward. Out of the corner of his eye he saw Troy rushing the net. Josh fired a pass over to him and it landed right on his stick. By now, Peter had gone to the net. Totally open, he banged his stick for Troy to give him a pass. But Troy tried to blast it with a snap shot. The goalie whipped his glove up and snatched the puck right out of the air. Angry that he had missed, Troy slammed his stick on the ice.

The whistle blew. Troy skated toward the bench. Josh didn't want to go in just yet. They'd only been out for twenty seconds.

"Why is he going in?" Peter asked.

"I don't know." Josh glanced toward the bench to see the next three forwards skating out for the face-off. Shrugging at Peter, Josh headed back to the bench.

When he got there, he stood beside Troy. "Why did you come in?" he asked.

"I'm tired. I think the sun zapped me."

"We were hardly in the sun," replied Josh. He hadn't come to this camp not to play. "Stay out next shift."

"Yeah, okay, whatever."

Suddenly the bench started cheering. Carl had scored. "Why couldn't I have got that goal?" said Troy. "I want to switch lines."

"Then ask Coach Manny if you can," said Josh, annoyed.

The next time Josh got on the ice he was determined to score. He lined up and clenched his mouth guard in his teeth. Troy lost the face-off, so Josh pushed his opposing winger to get to the puck. The guy pushed back. Josh shoved him again and barrelled forward. When he saw the puck heading toward the boards he wheeled over, angled his body, and laid a hit on the winger so hard the glass shook. The guy went down. The NHL Selects bench cheered.

Josh picked up the puck and stormed down the wing. He stayed wide, keeping his head up. Both Troy and Peter followed at a good clip. Peter, with his strong skating, was a few strides ahead of Troy, heading right to the net. Josh fired off a hard pass that landed on Peter's tape. Peter blasted off a shot that pinged the crossbar. The sound echoed through the arena. The puck flew up and over the net.

Josh sped behind the net and pushed the opposing defence against the boards. Playing scrappy hockey, he kept jabbing with his stick to get possession.

"Play the puck!" the ref yelled.

Josh drove his shoulder into the other player, wedging the puck between his skates to maintain possession. Peter came flying in for support and Josh pushed the puck with his foot toward him. Peter picked it up and swung around the net. He tried to tuck it under the goalie's pad, but somehow the goalie managed to hold the puck under his pad. The whistle blew.

"Nice try," said Josh to Peter.

"I was out front," said Troy.

"Yeah, and you were tied up," said Peter. "Get open next time."

Josh glanced at Troy. *Good for Peter for telling off Troy.*

Josh's line played one more whistle before they skated to the bench, exhausted.

"Good shift," said Gerald to Josh.

Josh didn't really feel as if it had been that great of a shift. Or at least, he didn't think *he'd* played that great. "Thanks," he replied.

For the rest of the game, Josh felt he played okay, but not great. The NHL Selects won 5–4. Peter had scored two of the goals but they were unassisted. Josh didn't pick up one point. In the dressing room, he undressed in silence.

"I keep telling myself," whispered Tony, "we've got lots of games left." Tony was short but thick, and played hard every single time he was on the ice. Sometimes, he had hands like cement when it came time to put the puck in the net, but no matter what, he kept trying and stayed positive. Josh admired him for that.

"I know," replied Josh. "But I hate it when I play like crap."

"There's another eight games. Remember what the motivational guy said: 'Don't hold on to anger. It just weighs you down.'"

Josh nodded. "You're right. We gotta move on and play better next time."

Sam leaned over and interrupted the conversation. "Hey, Wattie, you got your joke picked for tonight?"

Josh held up his thumb. "You bet."

At the post-game meal in the cafeteria, Kevin kept trying to get the attention of the blond girl. Josh had to admit, she was hot. She wore white shorts that showed off her tanned legs. He sure wouldn't have the guts to talk to her.

"Dude, she doesn't even notice you," said Steven.

"You wish. Watch, she'll notice." Kevin stood up.

"Look and learn." Kevin swaggered over and stood in front of the blond girl. The entire team was spread out on both sides of the long table. They could see him flick his bleached hair, but they couldn't hear what he was saying to her.

"He's probably asking her something stupid," said Steven.

"Oh yeah," said Sam. "Look at her face. She's not into him."

The girl frowned and shook her head. Then she turned on her heel and walked back into the kitchen.

"I think he got rejected big-time." Josh laughed, almost choking on his taco.

The rest of the team started laughing along with Josh.

When Kevin came back to the table, Steven said, "Jennings, you got burned."

Kevin swung his leg over the bench and sat back

down. "Yeah, well at least I've got the guts to try to talk to a hot girl."

"What are you talking about? I've got more guts than any of you." Troy stood up. Josh groaned. Leave it to Troy to try to outdo Kevin. "I'll go to the kitchen and talk to her. And I'll be smoo-ooth." Troy slid his hand slowly through the air.

"Go for it, Slippery," chortled Sam.

Kevin stood up. "Don't talk to her!"

"She's not yours, dude," said Troy, laughing.

Kevin leaned over, and it looked as if he might slug Troy.

Gerald, who was sitting at the next table with a few of the other counsellors, came over and put his hand on Troy's shoulder. "Troy, buddy, I don't think this is a good idea. No one needs to be going to the kitchen. They don't need some young guy with puppy-love drooling all over the food."

"He's the one with puppy-love." Troy pointed to Kevin and laughed again. The entire table burst out laughing too.

"Shut-up," said Kevin.

Troy shrugged off Gerald's hand and sat back down.

★ ★ ★

Back in the dorm room, Troy set up a movie for the guys on his DVD player, then picked up his deck of cards.

"I'm going next door to see the guys from Montana," he said.

Josh overheard Kevin say to Barry, "That guy is always going off."

"That's his problem," replied Barry. "Better the guys from Montana than us."

"You've got an hour, Troy," said Gerald. "And don't go anywhere else unless you tell me."

Troy smiled and saluted Gerald. "Yes, boss."

The hours sped by. Even after Troy came back and everyone had returned from the can and the lights were out, no one was ready to sleep.

Kevin asked, "Hey, isn't it joke night?"

"I did say that, didn't I?" said Gerald.

"You promised," said Josh.

"Okay, who wants to go first?"

Sam immediately piped up. "I got a Doctor, Doctor joke. Doctor, doctor, my kid just swallowed a pen, what should I do?" Sam paused a few seconds before giving the punch line. "Use a pencil until I get there."

Groans erupted.

"I've got one," said Josh over the noise. "What did they call Dracula when he won the playoffs?" Josh waited a few seconds to see if anyone knew the answer. Then he said, "The champire!"

"You guys from Alberta don't know how to tell jokes. I've got a redneck joke," said Carl.

"Cause you're from Saskatchewan, right?" said Steven.

"You bet," said Carl. "Okay, a redneck walks into a hardware store and wants a chainsaw that can cut six trees in an hour. The sales guy sells him the best model. The next day, the redneck comes back to the store and says, 'It only cut down one tree, and it took all day. Something's wrong with this stupid machine.' So the sales guy starts it up to see what's wrong, and the redneck says, 'What's *that* noise?!'"

Josh laughed.

"Does everyone get it?" Carl asked.

"Yeah, we get it," said Troy. "It's dumb."

"I thought it was funny," said Josh.

6 Skipping Out

Dressed in their shorts and running shoes, Josh, Sam, and Peter stood by the tournament stats board. They'd just finished lunch and had ten minutes before they had to meet in the field for dry-land.

"We're tied for first," Josh said, "with Team Switzerland."

Sam pointed to the board. "Yeah. We both have four points. I heard that the team we play tonight isn't too strong, which is such a bummer for me. Means no shots."

"Yeah, but you play in our game against Switzerland next Thursday." Josh playfully punched Sam on the shoulder. "That's when we'll really need you."

"Yeah, I figured that out too," said Sam. "I want to win that game."

"And we will," said Peter, butting in.

"Time to go, guys," yelled Gerald. "Bring your hats. It's going to be hot out there."

Josh was already wearing his Calgary Flames' cap.

Sam had donned his Ottawa Senators' cap and Peter's had an Edmonton Oilers' logo.

As he walked out to the field with Sam and Peter, the warm air circled Josh and he felt as if he was in a gigantic hot tub. The sun sat high in a perfect aqua sky; there wasn't a cloud in sight, not even one little white puff. The sweat dripped down Josh's forehead, and he wasn't even exercising yet. The heat went right through his T-shirt, seeming to sear his skin.

"I bet those tires could burn some real rubber now." Peter pointed to the black tires set up as part of the obstacle course.

"Too bad we can't drive yet," said Sam. "I can't wait to get my licence."

"I drive when I'm up north," said Peter.

"Where are you from again?" asked Carl. "I remember reading in *Hockey Now* that you're from someplace, like, crazy cold."

"Tuktoyaktuk," replied Peter.

"Do you like billeting in Edmonton?"

Peter shrugged. "Sometimes it sucks. But sometimes it's okay. I get to play on a good team."

"Okay, guys, listen up," said Gerald. "Here's what you have to do. And there's an Okanagan Hockey School T-shirt for whoever can do it the fastest. We're going to pull the tires from here to that post down there." Gerald pointed to a goalpost almost 15 metres away. "I'm going to time you. I want half the guys at this end and half at the other end. I'll number you off — one, two — and I want all the twos to go to the other end."

Josh was a one.

"Okay, get in line," said Gerald. He got out his stopwatch, pen, and clipboard. "Who wants to go first?"

Josh went to the head of the line, just to get it over with. After Gerald had strapped him in the harness, he walked to the goalpost. Gerald turned around and yelled, "Are you ready?"

"Yeah," shouted Josh, thinking he sounded a lot surer than he actually was.

"On your mark, get set, go!"

Josh took off. He pulled as hard as he could, the weight behind him heavy. The tires dragged. Josh started with long strides, but by the time he approached the post he was struggling with small, baby steps. And the closer he got, the smaller they got. Sweat poured down his face. His quadricep muscles screamed in pain.

"Come on," yelled Gerald. "You can do it."

"Go, Watson, go!" The guys started chanting.

Josh dug in, looking to the brown ground to make his last few steps. When he glanced up, he was only two steps away. He looked down again and grunted. Finally, he touched the post. He immediately bent over to catch his breath. His heart raced. His legs wobbled. He felt as if he might collapse, and he knew it had nothing to do with his diabetes. What a brutal exercise!

Gerald called out, "One minute, forty-eight seconds. Not bad."

Josh panted. "How many times did you say we're doing this?" His words came out in gasps.

"Three." Gerald smiled. "Just think how strong you'll be."

After everyone had gone once, Barry had made the fastest time. Josh thought Barry's legs looked the size of telephone posts, so it was no wonder he came first. Troy had the slowest time, and had almost fallen over at the end. Josh was surprised that Troy was so out of shape.

As Josh lined up to take his second turn, he saw Troy approach Gerald. They talked for a few seconds, then Troy left the group, obviously heading back to the room.

"What's up with him?" Josh heard Barry whisper to Carl.

"I was at the end when he finished and he said he had sunstroke. But I don't believe him," replied Carl. "The guy's always playing cards. He sucked in a new group last night."

"You ready, Josh?" Gerald yelled, drowning out the rest of the overheard conversation.

"Yup." Josh got in a runner's crouch so he could explode off the start this time.

By the end of the three tries, Josh had the fifth-best overall time on the team. He had been the most consistent with his three times, which really helped his score.

After they finished the tires, Gerald made them do a beep test, timed push-ups and sit-ups, and the medicine ball toss. Everything got recorded. Josh had top score in the sit-ups.

Even though Josh was exhausted by the end of the dry-land training, he stayed back to help Gerald clean up. As they walked back to the room, Gerald said, "You did a good job today. You won the sit-ups and did great on the tires all three times. It's like how you play hockey. You're pretty consistent for three periods." Gerald patted him on the back. "With your work ethic, you'll go a long way. And that counts a lot in the end, you know."

Josh looked up at Gerald, surprised at his encouraging words, and a bit embarrassed too. "Thanks," was all he could say.

"I'm looking forward to tonight's game," said Gerald.

"Yeah, me too," replied Josh.

Before the game, Josh sat beside Troy in the dressing room. He put on his shoulder pads. "How come you didn't do the rest of dry-land?"

"It's too hot to do that stuff outside."

"We were only out for an hour," said Josh. He paused. "Did you ask Coach Manny if you could switch lines yet?"

Troy shook his head. "I don't want to play with

Barry and Carl. They're losers."

Josh was glad Troy didn't switch lines because they started off, their first shift out, scoring a goal. Josh had passed the puck to Peter who, in an amazing pass, sent it to Troy at the side of the net. He flicked it up, making an amazing C-bar shot.

"Great goal!" Josh skated up to hug Troy.

"Thanks," said Troy. Then he turned to Peter. "Great pass."

Josh nodded his head in excitement. With Troy on board, their line could be unstoppable. Josh glanced at the bench. No one was coming out. He skated to centre ice to get ready for the face-off.

When the puck dropped, Troy battled with the other centre. Josh saw the scuffle and moved in to snatch the loose puck. Once it was on his stick, he looked up and saw Peter flying down the ice. Josh whipped off a bounce pass, hoping it would land where Peter could get it. The pass wasn't dead on, but Peter was moving with enough speed to pick it up and race toward the net. Since both Josh and Troy were still tied up, Peter was on his own. Josh broke away from the player who was holding him back and sped toward the net, hoping he might pick up a rebound. But Peter deked the goalie and roofed the puck. It sailed to the back of the net.

First shift and Josh's line had scored two goals already. As happy as Josh was about how well his line was playing, he was determined to get his first goal of the tournament. And he wanted it in this game.

Next out was the Barry–Carl–Kevin line. With his hand raised, Kevin skated over to Josh and Peter as they skated toward the bench.

"Awesome work, guys!" Kevin grinned as he slapped Peter's hand.

"It's your turn," said Josh. *And then it's mine*, he thought.

On the bench, Coach Manny said, "Now *that* shift was what I would call good team work."

Josh took his place on the bench. He leaned over to watch the Saskatoon boys light up the ice. "Man, they're good," said Peter, standing beside Josh.

"Yeah," said Josh. "They're in the same league as you." Then he glanced at Troy. "You too," he said.

"Thanks," replied Troy.

Troy never complimented Josh in return, but by this time Josh couldn't care less. He knew he was contributing as much as Troy to the team, if not more. Josh turned back to watch the game.

Barry picked up the puck along the boards. From the bench, Josh yelled, "Wheels, wheels."

Barry must have heard, because he lengthened his stride and pumped his legs, making use of his powerful stride.

"He's going to deke," said Josh.

"I think he'll rifle it from the hash marks," said Peter.

"I bet he roofs it with a wrist shot to the top corner," piped up Troy.

Barry deked and fired off a shot that went right through the goalie's five-hole. "I win," Josh said.

They had been out less than thirty seconds so Kevin, Barry, and Carl set up for the face-off. Josh knew that Kevin hadn't scored yet in the tournament, and he wondered if that was getting to him. In Kelowna, Kevin was one of the high-scorers on his team.

The puck dropped and Kevin batted it back. The defence picked it up and fired it up the boards. Barry picked it up and skated wide. Carl cut to the middle and skated with him, as Kevin moved forward on the other side. The defence on the other team, a big guy, tied up Carl. Josh could see that this team had a few really good defencemen. What they lacked was offence to put the puck in the net.

"Kevin's wide open," said Peter on the bench.

"Yeah, but I bet Barry doesn't pass to him," said Troy. "He's a selfish player."

Kevin banged his stick on the ice. Barry glanced quickly at him and passed the puck. Kevin one-timed it. The shot was hard and high, and the goalie didn't have a chance.

"That was a great pass," said Josh to Troy.

"Yeah, and it will probably be his one and only."

"Whatever," retorted Josh. "It's not as if you pass all the time either."

The NHL Selects won by a score of 13–3. Josh's line scored four of the goals. Josh did pick up a few more assists, and he knew that the points would be recorded on the camp website's stats page. But he still wished he would score a goal.

The team filed into the dressing room. When Josh took off his helmet the sweat poured from every hair on his head. He leaned back against the wall and smiled. Even though he didn't score a goal, he had to admit winning was fun.

"NHL Selects, meet back at the dorm," said Gerald, once everyone had changed into shorts, T-shirts, and flip-flops.

"I'm going to ask if we can go to that corner gas station," said Troy as they walked back to the dorm. "The Montana team was allowed to go there last night."

"Yeah," piped up Barry. "Let's see if we can get slushies."

"I don't have much money left," said Peter. "My dad is coming to Penticton tomorrow and he'll be at the game, so I can hit him up for more to hold me through the next week."

"I know a way you can make some money," said Troy. "Join the card game tonight."

Josh's stomach did a little flip. Make money playing cards?

"Don't do it," said Barry. "The guy is a shark."

Peter held up his hands. "I'll stick with asking my father. He'll give it to me. He always does."

Josh felt a little sick, and he knew it had nothing to do with his blood sugar. Troy was breaking one of the major camp rules by playing cards for money. How could he be so stupid? If anyone found out, Troy could be in big trouble. Would he bring the whole team down with him?

7 Quick Release

As much as he hated getting out of bed, Josh liked early morning ice the best. He slowly skated around and around, stretching with his stick behind his back. He inhaled and exhaled, enjoying the brisk air that pumped to his lungs. Arenas had a distinct smell — rubber and concrete and dry ice — and he loved it.

He concentrated on his skating stride and avoided thinking about Troy and his stupid card games. Josh had found Troy in the bathroom the night before, and tried to ask him about playing for money as they brushed their teeth. But Troy had just laughed at him and told him to relax.

Josh dug in his edges and picked up his pace. To heck with Troy. Josh wasn't going to let his cousin ruin his camp experience. Every day, Josh learned something new to help his game. It was time to stop thinking of Troy and focus on hockey. But what if Troy ruined everything for the team?

Forget Troy, Josh. Concentrate.

It took Josh three laps of skating and stretching to warm up. So far Coach Manny hadn't blown the whistle to call the team in for practice. Josh picked up a puck and carried it down the ice, stick-handling from side to side. The sound of his stick shifting the puck back and forth echoed off the concrete walls. He approached Sam in net and fired off a shot. Sam stuck up his glove hand and snagged it from the air. Then he threw it off to the side.

Josh glanced over at the bench. Coach Manny was still talking to Gerald. Josh skated around the back of the net and picked up another loose puck. He cradled the puck in his stick, pushing it forward. The familiar movement gave Josh an immediate rush of energy. Sure it was summer, and this was way too early to get up, but none of that mattered. This time Josh approached Zack, who was in net at the opposite end. He decided to try a "spinnerama" move he had seen Barry do. Josh cut to the outside, then pivoted his feet to spin his body around so his back was to the goalie. Then he circled the puck around his body and, as he turned to face Zack again, he tried to shoot the puck. The puck sailed wide of the net. Josh picked up the puck from behind the back of the net and skated down the ice. Again, he tried the same move, this time on Sam. It took five tries before Josh sunk the puck to the back of the net.

"Cool move, Wattie," said Sam.

* * *

After breakfast, they had headed off to skills training. Besides the practices and games, Josh liked the skills sessions best.

Skills training was located in a big warehouse building. Plexiglass covered the floor to simulate ice. Nets were lined up along the walls all the way around the rink, each covered by a shooter-tutor that covered the net, leaving five openings to shoot at.

Josh picked up a rubber ball from a bin and found a spot beside Peter. He tackled shooting and deking, trying to hit certain spots on the nets. Josh set up little games for himself to raise the stakes. *How many shots will it take to get a puck in all five holes?*

Josh aimed for the right top corner first and sunk the puck. He missed the left top corner, but sunk the puck in the five-hole that would be between the goalie's legs. Then he moved to the bottom corners. After nine shots he had got one in every hole. The day before, it had taken him only seven shots. So he tried again. And again. On his fifth go around, he sunk all five in seven shots.

He stopped to rest for a few seconds. Beside him, Peter was shooting like crazy. *That guy has a wicked shot*, thought Josh, proud to be playing on a team with his friend again.

"Top corner," said Josh to Peter.

Peter aimed for the top corner, and just missed.

"Five-hole," said Josh.

This time Peter sank the puck in the net.

Josh kept calling out spots for Peter to aim for. After Peter had dropped in ten, he stopped. "How many?" he asked, wiping away the sweat dripping off his brow with his bare arm.

"You made ten in thirteen."

"Cool. Yesterday it took me fourteen to get ten. Your turn."

Josh got into position. As soon as Peter called a spot, Josh made his shot. He counted to himself and, when he had sunk ten, he stopped. "How many?"

"Thirteen." Peter grinned. "We're tied."

Josh smiled. Things were looking up. "Sweet. I can't wait to play tonight."

"Montana is supposed to be pretty good," said Peter.

"Yeah, although I heard their goalie isn't great. Massive five-hole."

Peter grinned. "I heard that too." He started stick-handling the puck. "From now on, let's just play a five-hole game so we can each score a hat-trick tonight. And we need to work on surprising the goalie. We need to work on perfect aim."

"And quick release, right?"

"Yeah."

"I always get caught holding the puck for too long before shooting," said Josh. "Then I lose it."

"The trick is to pick your spot while you're still skating, hold the spot in your mind, and do a quick release while in stride. If you stop skating, then pick your spot, there's the chance of a turnover. And it's harder to surprise the goalie."

Josh nodded, knowing Peter's tips would take a lot of practice, but that it would be worth it.

★ ★ ★

In the afternoon, the NHL Selects were scheduled to float down the famous Penticton canal. People from all over the world vacationed in Penticton because the town was set in between two big lakes — Lake Okanagan and Skaha Lake. A canal connected the two lakes. Tourists and locals floated down the canal on all kinds of blow-up toys, air mattresses, and inner tubes.

At the start, close to Lake Okanagan, Josh and his teammates were able to rent black inner tubes. All the way down, Josh splashed and dumped all his friends and teammates — all but Troy. Gerald had made him come along but he was miserable the entire time so he floated by himself.

The canal took less time than Gerald had anticipated because the water was flowing faster than usual. This was a huge bonus, because when they got back to the dorm they had time to rest. Josh plopped down on his bed and fell asleep right away.

When he woke, it was already time for dinner. He sat up and rubbed his eyes. Again when he looked around he noticed that Troy was missing. Was he out playing cards again?

"Time for dinner, guys." Gerald's voice boomed. "Then it's game time!"

Josh, Sam, Peter, Steven, and Kevin walked over to the cafeteria together. Troy came running to catch up to them. He was out of breath.

"Where were you, Slippery?" Sam asked.

"Talking to the Montana guys."

Talking, right, thought Josh.

"I hope you didn't give them our game plan," said Kevin.

"I'm starving," said Peter. "Does anyone know what the mystery meat in those sandwiches was yesterday? They were gross."

"They weren't that bad," said Kevin. "I think Natalie helped make them."

"Natalie?" Josh was surprised. "Did you talk to her?"

Kevin jerked his head to flick his hair out of his eyes. "Not yet. But soon."

"Then how do you know her name?"

"Duh, it's not hard to find out a chick's name. Or her age."

"If she made the sandwiches yesterday and the eggs this morning, she's not a very good cook," said Peter.

"Kevin's in love," mocked Sam. "So, how old is she?"

Kevin flexed his arm muscles. "Sixteen."

"Sixteen!" Josh burst out laughing. "You've got to be kidding."

"Dude, she's two years older than you," said Sam. He doubled over in laughter. "Get a life, man. She won't have anything to do with you."

"Yeah," said Troy as they pushed their way through the arena doors and toward the cafeteria. "She needs a real man — like me."

"Just you wait and see." Kevin flexed again. "With these babies, I'm her man."

"I wonder what's for dinner tonight," said Troy as he butted into the cafeteria line in front of Josh.

"It could be crap, but if *Nat-a-lie* is cooking, Kevin will think it's amazing," Sam snorted.

"Shut-up." Kevin jumped on Sam's back.

Gerald raised his eyebrows and shook his head at the silly antics. "Get off him, Loverboy."

All the guys started laughing and chanting, "Lover-boy! Loverboy!"

8 Holding Back

When the puck dropped, the speed started. Coach Manny had not exaggerated — Montana had fast skaters. From the bench, Josh watched the play go up and down the ice at a furious pace. Barry and Carl were on fire, and Kevin was keeping up and then some. Kevin flew around the back of the net and picked up the puck. He snapped off a perfect pass, landing the puck on Barry's stick. Wide-open, Barry one-timed it and sent it right to the back of the net.

As the NHL Selects on the bench cheered, the line skated over to them.

"We're on," said Troy. He blasted onto the ice. Josh followed, with Peter right behind him.

After the face-off and a scramble at centre, the puck flew along the boards. Troy skated over to pick it up, and Peter rushed in for support. Josh tried to stay open, leaving Troy someone to pass to. He tapped his stick on the ice. If Troy could send him a pass, Josh could pick it up and dump the puck.

Although Troy fought hard, Montana fought harder. They were really jabbing at him. Troy tried to keep the puck along the boards by putting his skates in a V and holding it in between, but the ref yelled, "Play the puck!"

In frustration, a Montana player shoved Troy hard off the puck. Then their forward, also along the boards, flipped the puck out to a winger in the middle of the ice, who took off toward the NHL Selects net.

Josh put on the brakes and pivoted to change direction. He tried to back-check, but the Montana forward who had the puck was fast. Josh's legs burned. He kept striding. One stride. Two strides. There was no way he could out-skate his opponent, so he tried to angle him into the boards. A stronger skater than Josh, Peter had made up a few strides and was almost on the Montana forward. Peter tried to lift the Montana player's stick, but the player stayed just out of reach and made a backhand pass that landed on his winger's stick. The winger one-timed it. It hit Zack's shoulder and bounced into the net. Zack slammed his stick on the ice in frustration. Josh sighed, but then gently tapped Zack's pads. "Shake it off," he said. Zack lowered his head and shook it, swinging his long hair from side to side.

Shoulders slumped, Josh skated to the bench. He hated being out when goals were scored against his team. It gave him a lousy plus-minus record.

"Nice skate," said Coach Manny to Peter. "You almost had him."

"Good try," Gerald said to Josh. "Remember what the power skating instructor said about explosiveness. You can do it, you have the technique."

Josh nodded his head. Did Gerald really think he had good skating technique?

When Troy came off, Coach Manny patted his shoulder and said, "I want to show you something." He got out his white board and a black marker.

Josh took his position beside Peter on the bench.

"They're after Troy," Peter said to Josh. "I wonder why. He must have rubbed them the wrong way."

Josh pursed his lips to hold his words inside. Josh thought he knew why they were out to get Troy. He felt Troy's shoulder rubbing his shoulder pad.

"Why did I get the white board routine? Next time support me," he said to Josh.

Josh just glared at Troy in response.

The rest of the period was no better. Troy's head wasn't in the game. He made one mistake after another and he didn't seem to care. Montana capitalized on every slip he made, and crushed him every chance they had. *The guy has so much talent,* Josh thought. *Why is he wasting it?* Josh was ready to blow up at his cousin.

Partway through the third period, the score was tied 3–2 for Montana. Peter had scored one of the goals for the NHL Selects unassisted, but otherwise Josh's line had no points. On the bench, Josh gritted his teeth and mumbled to Peter, "Troy's not pulling his weight."

Peter looked over to where Troy was sitting on the bench. Every time he came in he sat instead of stood.

Gerald looked down the bench to where Josh and Peter were standing, ready to take their shift. "Josh, your line is next. Get ready."

Josh turned to Troy. "Troy, we're out!"

"Cool it, I've got time. Those guys just went out."

Josh's face felt hot. He could feel his blood racing through his body. "You're so lazy, Troy! Why did you come to this camp if you're not going to play?"

Troy stood up slowly, glaring at Josh. "I've got more points than you. You're one of the worst scorers on this team."

"Shut-up."

"You're just jealous because you're not as good as me."

Something inside Josh snapped. He pushed Troy, who stumbled, knocking over the water bottles sitting on the bench.

Gerald immediately stepped in between them. "Can it, guys. Or I'll sit you both."

Ready at the gate, and staying out of the confrontation, Peter turned and said, "Come on, we're out!" He flew on the ice and Josh followed.

Josh was so angry that, every chance he got, he nailed a player from the Montana Team. He kept hitting and hitting, trying to free the puck along the boards. Then he saw Troy go to the bench. He didn't want to go off just because Troy was tired. Peter was still out and the whistle hadn't blown yet. Josh saw Kevin come out to replace Troy. In mid-stride, Kevin got a lucky bounce and managed to pick up the puck. Josh rushed with him. Together they flew down the ice, heading toward the net on a two-on-one. When they were in front of the net, Josh tapped his stick. Kevin fired the puck over to him and Josh one-timed it, smoking it to the back of the net.

Yes! His first goal of the tournament! And he had tied the game! Josh pumped his arm. Kevin and Peter rushed over. Peter pulled on Josh's cage, looked him in the eyes and said, "You drilled that sucker."

Josh grinned. Then Peter and Josh skated off. As they took their places on the bench, Josh really wanted to tell Troy to take that and stick it. But he didn't. He didn't want to get benched.

The two teams battled until the buzzer sounded. The game ended in a tie. In the dressing room, Josh refused to talk to Troy. He knew he would just say something he shouldn't. Coach Manny told the team that they hadn't played their best game, but to let this one slide off their backs — they couldn't let it affect their play for the rest of the tournament. Josh felt a lot of the trouble they'd had was because Troy was dogging it, and had somehow fired up the Montana team to play hard hockey.

Josh was still angry when he headed out of the dressing room. "Let it go," said Peter in his low voice.

"Yeah, Josh, just let it go," said Sam, on Josh's other side. "If we have to meet that team again, we'll kill them."

"It bugs me that Troy doesn't care."

"That's not your problem," said Peter.

"It is when I'm on a line with him. And I'm the one who asked him to come to this camp." Josh blew out a rush of air. Peter patted him on the back and Josh felt his body lose some of its tension. Sam and Peter were right. Holding on to anger off the ice wouldn't do him any good.

After the game, Gerald took the NHL Selects to the gas station convenience store to get some junk food. Josh stayed clear of Troy, walking far behind him. At the store, Josh searched the shelves of candy and chips, trying to figure out what he wanted. He knew he couldn't eat as much junk food as the other guys because of his diabetes. He picked up a little plastic bag and the plastic tongs, deciding that he'd get a bag of mixed candy. He could take it on the bench for when his blood sugar got too low. He had just put seventy-five cents' worth of candy in his bag when he heard the store's bell tinkle. He looked up to see some of the players from the Montana team entering the store.

Josh was reaching in for some spearmint leaves when he overheard one of the Montana players say, "Look at how much hotshot is getting."

Josh glanced down the aisle to see who they were talking about. Troy was standing at the till with an armful of candy and snacks.

"That guy thinks he's so good," said one of the Montana teammates.

Josh ducked his head so they wouldn't know he was listening to their conversation.

"My dad is going to kill me when I ask for more money."

"You have to. You can't keep borrowing from everyone else."

"I know. I just wish that idiot hadn't taken it all on me. I swear he cheats."

At the till, Troy finished paying, then he turned to catch Josh's eye. When Troy saw the Montana guys huddled near Josh, he held up his bags of junk food and said in a loud voice, "Don't buy anything, Josh. I can share with you."

"It's okay," replied Josh, embarrassed by the looks he got from the Montana players. "I've got my own bag of candy." Josh moved past Troy and headed to the till.

"I'll wait for you outside," said Troy.

"Don't bother," Josh whispered under his breath.

Josh gave the cashier his money, and hurried out of the store. He breathed deeply when he stepped outside.

As the NHL Selects headed back to the dorm in a loose pack, Troy fell into step beside Josh. Josh ate a gummy worm, ignoring Troy.

Troy lifted up his bag of candy. "I've got enough to share with everyone. That's why I bought it."

Josh eyed Troy. Since they were little, Troy had always been generous. When Josh had visited him in the summers, Troy had always let him play with his toys. Then when they got older, he never hogged the computer or his video games. But until now, Josh had never seen how Troy used his stuff to make people like him. Troy always had to show that somehow he was better than everyone else. For the first time, Josh felt a little sorry for his cousin.

"Sam will eat it," muttered Josh. "Or Peter," he added in a louder voice, "if you tell him it's pizza."

Everyone laughed, and some of the tension eased.

9 Poetry in Motion

Josh woke up the next morning to find everyone laughing at him. He examined his hand suspiciously. No shaving cream.

"What's wrong with you guys?" He picked up the bag with his bathroom stuff in it.

Sam wound up a towel and whipped Josh on the leg. "Hey," yelled Josh, chasing him into the washroom.

When he looked at himself in the mirror, he groaned. Hearts drawn in black ink were all over his face. *Wattie* was written on his forehead.

Sam was laughing so hard he was doubled up in the corner by the showers.

Troy cruised into the washroom. "Told you I'd get you back for the shaving cream trick."

Josh tried to get a read on Troy. Had he played the prank to be mean? Or was he honestly trying to fit in with the team?

Josh tried to douse Troy with water but ended up

spilling it on the floor. Then he chased Troy and Sam out of the washroom. They fell on their beds laughing.

★ ★ ★

At lunch, Sam leaned over and whispered to Josh, "Kevin's all goo-goo eyes again. And Troy's making a big play for Natalie just to make him mad. Let's help Loverboy get an advantage."

Josh wanted to help Kevin, if for no other reason than to get back at Troy. Josh knew that Troy didn't really have any interest in Natalie; he was just trying to outdo Kevin. Troy's teamwork and good attitude hadn't even lasted the morning. He was back to his old tricks of trying to one-up everyone. Josh wished he hadn't invited his cousin to the camp.

Josh nodded and whispered back, "We could write a poem for her and sign it from Kevin. That would make him the man, for sure."

"You're such an English geek. But it's a good idea. Come on, let's go in the hall. Grab a napkin."

Josh stuffed his napkin in his pocket and followed Sam out the door. Peter was in the hallway, heading into the cafeteria.

"What are you guys doing? Is lunch really that awful?"

"This is going to be so funny," said Sam. "Troy and Kevin are both after Natalie. We're going to write a poem and give it to Natalie and tell her it's from Kevin."

"We want Kevin to win this one," said Josh. "Otherwise we can't call him Loverboy anymore."

"A poem?" Peter's eyes widened. "Like English homework? You've got to be kidding me."

"Don't worry," said Sam to Peter. "This will work. Josh is a brainiac at English. How should we start it, Josh?"

"Okay, how about, *Roses are red, violets are blue. You're so cute that I love you*?"

"Come on, be serious. Just because we put hearts all over you face doesn't mean you can go all sappy on us. We can't put *lo-o-o-ve* in it."

Josh put his hand to his face. All day he'd been razzed about it. Even Coach Manny had commented that his face might need a better wash.

"Yeah, and the hearts should give you inspiration to write a good poem," said Peter.

"All right," said Josh. "I'll do this to help Loverboy." Josh closed his eyes to think. Then he opened them and said, "Here goes."

Sam poised his pen on the napkin. "You recite, I'll write."

Josh formed the words in his mind before he started.

"*Like a summer breeze,*
You swept into the room,

Your hair swirling
around your face.
Then you looked up
And smiled
like the sun on a beautiful warm day.
My only thought
Was to smile back."

"Holy, that's good!" said Peter. "But it doesn't rhyme."

"Poetry doesn't have to rhyme," said Josh.

"Josh, that's awesome," said Sam. He looked at Peter. "Told you he was a brainiac."

"Do you think it's too good?" Peter asked.

"No. Even if she figures out that Loverboy Kevin didn't write it himself, she'll be impressed. At least Troy won't stand a chance," said Josh.

"Now all we need is a delivery boy," said Sam. He tried to hand the napkin to Peter.

"No way," said Peter, shaking his head. "I'm not giving it to her." He backed up and gestured with his hands, making it clear that he wanted no part of the scheme.

"Me either," replied Josh. "I wrote it."

"Wimps." Sam folded the napkin in half. "I'll do it." He headed back into the cafeteria, grinning from ear to ear.

★ ★ ★

That night they were playing Team Canada, a team that had won only one game in the first week of the tournament. Josh hoped that it would be his day to pick up a few more points. He stepped on the ice to warm up, trying to skate with confidence, but the ice was a bit mushy. He figured it was because they were playing the early game when the sun was at its hottest. The temperature outside was scorching, over forty degrees.

Troy skated beside him. "Let's kick some butt tonight."

Josh held up his hand and Troy punched his glove. Earlier in the day they'd all gone to the driving range. While the rest of the team had hit golf balls, Troy had slept in a plastic lawn chair. Josh didn't care where Troy slept, as long as he came to the games ready to play. This would be their fifth game in five nights.

Their line was up first. Josh took to the red line. The puck dropped and Troy easily won the face-off. He batted it over to Peter. Peter picked up the puck and sped down the ice, his strides powerful and quick. Josh followed, working to keep up with him. Being on a line with Peter was making Josh a better skater. Once they hit the blue line, Josh charged to the net.

Josh had been working all week on keeping his

feet moving at all times. He had noticed that Peter never stopped moving his feet the entire shift. Coach Manny had been helping Josh during the practice sessions, teaching him to give-and-go at all times. Every time he released a pass he needed to move to open ice. Standing still wasn't an option.

When Josh was at the ringette line, Peter nailed a pass to him. The puck landed on Josh's tape. Right away, he took one long stride, then in mid-stride he flipped up the puck, aiming to hit the open side of the net. The goalie shuffled across the net, but didn't get there in time. The puck landed, dribbled, and went just centimetres over the red goal line. The ref put his hand down, signalling the goal was in. Josh jumped in the air, running on his skates.

Josh raced over to Peter. "Awesome pass."

"You were there. That was a nice move. You were kind of like ... a poem in motion." Peter grinned.

Josh grinned back at Peter. Poetry in motion. He liked that.

By the end of the first period the score was 4–0 for the NHL Selects. Peter had put in an unassisted goal, and Barry and Carl had each scored. At the bench, Coach Manny gathered the players. "I know the ice is soft today, but that means you have to dig a little deeper. This team has struggled a bit all week, but sometimes they come back pretty good. Don't let up."

First shift out in the second period, Team Canada

fired the puck from the blue line. Sam caught it and threw it out, but it took a bad bounce and ended up in front of the net. The Team Canada forward slapped at it and the puck slid right past Sam. Sam looked behind him, confused. Josh knew that Sam never let in goals like that.

From the bench, Josh yelled, "Shake it off, Slammer."

Sam lifted his cage and swigged some water.

Every shift out, Josh tried to replicate his goal, but he just couldn't get it in the net again. Peter managed to score two unassisted goals by just picking up the puck and going end-to-end. Barry and Carl scored a goal each. Kevin managed to sink one from an amazing pass from Carl.

Josh looked at the clock as he faced off. Just four minutes left to play, and the score was 9–1. Sam hadn't let in another goal. But he hadn't had to stop many either.

The puck dropped. Peter picked it up and sent it back to the defence. Josh skated up his wing, looking for a pass. Sure enough, the defence sent it up the boards. Josh picked it up and headed to the net. Out of the corner of his eye he saw Peter zooming to the goal. Josh made the pass and headed to the side of the net to catch a possible rebound. Peter wound up for a slapshot, but instead of shooting on the goalie he sent the puck to Josh. Josh one-timed it and hit the post.

Peter picked it up and rifled off another shot. This time the goalie deflected it right out front, centimetres away from Josh's stick. Josh fired it off again, hitting another post. The puck zinged out and back into play. A player from Team Canada picked it up and skated out past the blue line.

Josh smacked his stick on the ice, clenched his teeth, and back-checked, skating through the fatigue in his legs. He managed to catch the guy, wrapping his stick around him, trying to create a turnover. Without even thinking, he grabbed the guy's shirt with his free hand. He had to stop him.

Then he heard the whistle blow.

The ref looked at him and made the motion for a holding penalty.

Josh blew out a rush of air. He knew the ref was right. He had held the guy. Josh skated to the penalty box.

He leaned back in the box and tried to forget about how he'd missed two open nets and hit two posts. Josh served his two minutes. When his time was up, Coach Manny waved him over to the bench.

"You outskated him, Josh," he said. "You don't need to hold. Have confidence that you can beat him."

Josh nodded. With the game almost out of time, Josh had only one more shift. When he stepped on the ice, Peter skated to the face-off with him. "I'll set you up," he said.

Josh thought that Peter was not only the best player Josh had ever played with, he was the most unselfish.

As soon as the puck dropped, it seemed to bounce everywhere. Peter pushed and shoved, but he couldn't get his stick on it and it skidded out of reach. Josh hustled, hoping to pick it up and pop another one in the net, but then the buzzer went.

After the end-of-the-game goalie congrats, they all headed to the dressing room.

"No games on the weekend, guys," said Coach Manny. He held up his hands. Josh noticed how big they were. He had heard when he played in the NHL, he had been super tough. "But get ready for next week," continued Coach Manny. "We start back on Monday, and we're going to do some serious damage."

"We still have to play Switzerland," said Carl.

"Yes, and they're good," said Coach Manny. "Not a loss yet. But that's because they haven't played us."

Troy leaned over to Josh. "I think it's time I made friends with the Swiss guys."

Josh frowned. "Don't do that. You keep doing what you're doing, and you could get our team kicked out of this tournament."

"I won't get you and your team kicked out," said Troy sarcastically.

Josh shook his head at Troy. "It's *our* team, bonehead."

10 Holding All the Cards

Josh decided that Troy could do whatever he wanted on the weekend. Josh was sick of constantly trying to figure out his cousin. He was going to catch up on his sleep and spend some quality time with his friends. The days were still jammed with activities but, because there were no games to prep for, everything and everyone seemed to move at a slower pace.

"Let's go to the concession," said Sam after a soccer game, flinging his T-shirt over his bare back.

"Sure," said Josh. He tossed his T-shirt on his head to get some shade.

Sam smelled his armpit. "I need to get a clean T-shirt first, though. I've worn this one all week and it stinks."

"That's disgusting," said Peter. "Why have you worn the same shirt?"

"I dunno," replied Sam. "Who cares? My mom's not here."

At the concession Peter ordered two slices of pizza.

"Hey, dude," said Kevin. "Do you have any money left?"

Peter grinned and shrugged. "My dad gave me more."

"Are you going to save some of your cashola to buy Natalie a goodbye present?" Sam asked Kevin as he butted in front of him in line.

Kevin pushed Sam behind him. "Who says it's going to be goodbye?"

"Hey," said Troy, in line behind Kevin. "You're not butting in front of me." He jokingly pushed Sam and cut ahead of all of them. Then he approached the counter. "How much money do I have left?" Troy asked the girl working the concession. "I want to get a really nice goodbye present for a girl."

Josh stopped fooling around to listen. Good thing Kevin wasn't paying attention and hadn't heard Troy's plan. Josh knew that Kevin actually really liked Natalie, and that Troy probably just wanted her to say he got her, like she was a prize or something. But Troy was the one with the money and the plan, so maybe the odds were in his favour.

The girl looked up Troy's account sheet in a binder. "You still have just over two hundred dollars," she said.

"I want to take out a hundred."

"How do you have so much money left?" Josh

asked as Troy pocketed the money.

"I just do," Troy retorted, and walked away.

★ ★ ★

On Sunday afternoon, Josh had time to finish reading *The Thief Lord*. Troy was off making friends with every team, asking them all to play cards. Josh tried not to care.

As the team walked into the cafeteria for dinner that night, Josh whispered to Sam, "Hey look, Natalie's in the kitchen."

"I wonder if she'll say anything to him about the poem," said Sam.

"She keeps looking this way. I wonder if she thinks one of us is Kevin," Josh whispered.

Once he had his plate of food, Josh forgot about Natalie. He hunkered over his mashed potatoes and beef, eating one forkful after another without a break. The drink and snack from earlier hadn't come close to filling him up. He had his head down when Sam elbowed him in the ribs. "Look who's coming."

Josh looked up. "It's Natalie. She's walking over here!"

He noticed that Troy sat up straighter and started to talk in a loud voice about how many goals he was going to score in the second week of the tournament. Now that Natalie was actually close, Kevin did the exact opposite, looking down at his plate and pushing the food around. Was Loverboy Kevin nervous? That would be a first.

"Hi, guys," Natalie said sweetly. "Which one of you is Kevin?"

Smirking, Barry stood up and pointed to Kevin. "He's your man!"

"Um, thanks for the poem, Kevin. It was really sweet. And so good. You're a really good poet."

"Sweet?" Carl burst out laughing. Then he turned to Kevin. "Loverboy, did you send the chick poetry?"

Kevin's face turned four shades of red. Steven lightly pounded his back. "Here, let's get the puck out of your throat, big guy."

Josh noticed that Natalie was starting to look confused and a little embarrassed. Kevin must have seen it too. He slapped Steven's hand away and stood up. He smiled and the red began to leave his face.

"You're welcome, Natalie," said Kevin. "It was my pleasure."

Josh was amazed. Only Kevin could recover that quickly. He had confidence in spades.

Natalie lifted her hand and gave Kevin a little wave. "I have to get back to work." She smiled. "Come talk to me later, okay?"

"Thanks for the poem," Barry said in a high, squeaky voice once Natalie was out of earshot. "It was so-o-o-o sweet."

"Poetry, dude?" Carl laughed. "You've got to be kidding me."

"Thanks so much, Kevy, for the wonderful poem." Steven pretended to swoon.

"Yeah, well," said Kevin, standing up, "I didn't see her ask any of you to come and see her afterward, now did I?" Kevin picked up his dirty dishes and left the table.

"Hey, Troy," said Josh. "She didn't even glance your way."

"Yeah, well. She's not my type."

"Sucks to lose, doesn't it, Troy?" said Barry.

"I never liked her anyway." Troy left his tray and strutted out of the cafeteria, smiling at every girl except for Natalie.

Peter turned to Sam and Josh. "Man, nothing phases Kevin. We should all take lessons from that guy."

"It was my poem," groaned Josh. "I could have got the girl!"

Sam patted him on the back. "It takes more than poetry, Wattie. If I were you, I'd stick to hockey."

Josh grinned, knowing that Sam had just complimented his hockey and ... he could have, maybe, got the girl. After all, it was his poem.

11 Scrappy Hockey

"Okay, guys, ice is ready," said Gerald.

The team filed out of the dressing room. Peter turned to Josh and said, "Let's kick some butt. Let's beat Team World."

"First shift, we're scoring," said Josh.

The puck dropped to start the game and Peter battled for it. Few players could knock him off his stick. Josh flew up his wing, hoping to get a pass. But the puck went over to Troy's side. Troy picked it up and skated wide. Josh straddled the blue line until Troy was over, then he drove to the net. Instead of passing, Troy took a shot. The puck rebounded out and whizzed by Josh. He reached but couldn't get his stick on it. A player from Team World picked it up, but Peter pivoted and raced after him, catching him before he got out of the zone. Peter lifted the opponent's stick and pushed him off the puck. Then he turned and fired off a shot that was so hard it zinged past the goalie.

Josh skated over to him. "Great shot."

Peter just nodded.

The score remained 1–0 for the rest of the period. The NHL Selects had a lot of chances, but they just couldn't seem to bury the puck. Carl hit the post twice. Every time Barry fired off his wicked slapshot he managed to just miss the net. Peter, Josh, and Troy hustled and worked to keep the puck in; they were successful at that but not at getting another goal.

Josh was starting to get frustrated, but then he remembered what Coach Manny had told him about having confidence in himself and not resorting to holding. He could see that Team World was having trouble keeping up, and so they played sticky hockey and did a lot of holding. The refs seemed oblivious.

At the end of the period, Josh glanced up at the scoreboard before he joined the rest of the team gathered around Coach Manny.

"Keep shooting, guys," said Coach Manny. "Law of averages says it will go in if you keep shooting."

In the second period the NHL Selects did keep shooting, but nothing showed on the scoreboard. Barry came off his shift and slammed his stick. "These guys are cheap shots and they're really starting to bug me. I wish they'd stop holding. That last guy grabbed my jersey. The ref isn't calling anything on them."

"They're a bunch of hackers," said Carl.

Josh's line was out next. He skated toward the face-off

zone, telling himself he was going to get a goal. As soon as the puck dropped, he moved. But then he felt a stick across his body. He shoved the stick away, but the Team World player grabbed Josh's stick with his free hand. Frustrated, Josh shoved him. The player fell to the ice. Josh heard the whistle. The ref was pointing at Josh.

"Two minutes for roughing."

"What? He was holding," Josh muttered under his breath.

Josh could hear his teammates on the bench yelling, "Watch the holding, ref." Shaking his head, Josh skated toward the bench.

Josh sat down and watched Troy and Peter play short-handed. They played hard and Peter just kept icing the puck.

At the line change, Barry and Carl took to the ice. Josh could tell that Barry was steaming mad by the way he chopped at the Team World guys. Suddenly, Barry overturned the puck and was about to head on a breakaway, when a World player held out his arm to hold him back. Barry turned around and punched him. The whistle blew. Josh groaned. Barry had just got them another penalty. Barry argued with the ref for a few seconds before he headed toward the penalty box. When the gate opened Barry threw his stick.

"This is crap," he said to Josh. "They hold and we get the penalties."

"The ref's not calling anything on them," said Josh. "Just us."

"Troy knew they were going to play dirty and sneaky before we started this game. The guy's such a jerk."

"What are you talking about?" Josh asked, confused. What did Troy have to do with this game?

"Your cousin plays cards with everyone. When they lose to him, he takes all their money and they get totally cranked and play hack hockey. This team told me to warn him they were going to get revenge. And they are. Troy is giving our whole team a bad reputation."

Josh gritted his teeth and remained silent as the time ticked off on his penalty. As he stepped out of the box he looked for a signal from Coach Manny. He was called over to the bench.

The rest of the period was a gong show. The ref dished out one penalty after another to the NHL Selects. At one point, Josh looked over to see three of his teammates in the box.

In the middle of the third period, the NHL Selects were two players down, and Josh was on the ice with just Troy and a defence in a three-against-five when the puck ended up in front of their net. Josh played the triangle, swatting his stick on the ice to keep the puck away from Zack. Team World cycled the puck, and Josh couldn't get near it to clear it down the ice. Team

World moved closer and closer to the net. Josh kept slapping, hoping to intercept the puck and send it down. When the puck went to the corner, Josh skated forward a few steps, hoping to set a trap and have the World player make a bad pass, but the puck was lofted over his stick. Another Team World player picked it up and fired a low shot that slipped under Zack's pads.

Josh shook his head. Man, he really hated ending up with a bad plus-minus for the game. If the stupid ref wasn't handing out so many penalties the goal wouldn't have happened. If Troy wasn't acting like such an idiot this wouldn't have happened.

The rest of the game didn't get any better. Josh's team spent all their energy killing penalties. The game ended in a tie. The score didn't reflect how well either team played. What a joke.

In the NHL Selects dressing room, everyone grumbled and complained. Now they had two ties, and couldn't afford even one loss. They would have to beat Switzerland to make it to the gold-medal game.

"We lost because of the stupid reffing," said Troy.

Coach Manny held up his hand. "I'll agree the reffing was bad," he said, "but you guys also didn't handle the situation very well. You retaliated and created even more penalties. You've still got two more games before the final medal game. Shake off this game. It's history, and you have to focus on winning the next two."

"Yeah, and one is against Switzerland," said Kevin. "We're going to own them."

"You will need to play hard," said Coach Manny. "They're fast and skilled. You have to show up with the right attitude and some discipline. You need to execute your breakout next game, instead of getting yourself caught along the boards in scrums that end in penalties. Use your speed and skill. I heard Wayne Gretzky once say, 'Trying is for losers, execution is for winners.' What you need to do now is forget, focus, and execute."

"I don't know about everyone else, but I'm sure looking forward to a good game. I can't wait to play Switzerland," said Troy.

"That's the spirit," said Coach Manny. "You're not out yet. Get some sleep tonight, guys." With that, he left.

Troy turned to Josh and whispered, "Seriously. I can't wait to play Switzerland. I met some of them today. They're so cocky. They told me they'll beat us for sure." He smirked. "I'm going to beat them for sure."

"Uh, Troy, we're a team," said Josh, throwing his shin pad in his bag. "I think you should say *we'll* beat them."

"I'm not talking about on the ice, if you know what I mean," retorted Troy.

"I know exactly what you're talking about. On

and off the ice, you're making us lose." Josh tore off his elbow pads and threw them in his bag. "If you're not going to play by the rules, why don't you just go home and let us win?"

12 Fired Up

Josh lined up at the end zone for the skills testing session. Four stations had been set up around the rink: an accuracy shooting station, a speed shooting station, and two skating stations, one for short distance and the other for long distance. Josh's first station was the speed shooting station.

His first shot was the wrist shot. Usually his wrist shot was his best. He faced the net.

"Whenever you're ready," said the head instructor, checking Josh's name on the clipboard. Another instructor stood behind the net with a radar gun.

Josh nodded. Then he sucked in a deep breath before he wound up for his shot.

"Fifty-five miles per hour," yelled the instructor with the radar gun.

Next in line was Peter. His shot got clocked at 60

mph, only five higher than Josh.

After everyone had done the wrist shot three times, each player's fastest shot was recorded. The head instructor called out, "Okay, guys. Slapshot is next."

Behind Josh, Peter said, "I'm going to blast it."

Josh wanted to blast it too. When it was his turn, he stepped up to the line, wound up, and fired it as hard as he could.

"Sixty-nine," yelled the instructor.

Josh thought that was pretty good until Peter fired off a shot that was clocked at 85 mph.

"There are guys in Juniors that can't shoot that hard," said Josh to Peter.

Peter shrugged. "I had a coach this year who taught me the proper mechanics. It really helps. You have to lean into it."

When the whistle blew, Josh and Peter headed over to skating. The first race was a 30-metre forward race. Josh knew he wouldn't win this race. He just didn't have the explosive power off the start. He figured that the winner would be either Peter or Barry. Josh wanted to excel and put his all in the skating tests, but he didn't do well on any of them.

"You're up, Josh," said Peter at the accuracy shooting station. Josh studied the net covered with a shooter-tutor, debating in his head which shot to go for first. He had only six shots to get as many of the holes as he could, and he had to call out the spot he was aiming for each time.

"Remember, pick your spot. Hold the picture in your mind, then go for the quick release," whispered Peter.

"Where are you going first?" asked the instructor.

"Left corner," Josh said.

Yes! His first shot hit the hole and disappeared.

"Right corner," he said. He wound up and missed. Now he only had four shots left to hit four spots. "Five-hole," he said. The puck hit dead on. "Right corner," he said again. He got that one in too.

Josh had two shots left and two spots left. Both were on the bottom, Josh's weak area. "Right bottom," he called out. He sucked in a deep breath, took his time, and shot the puck to the low right corner. It went in. *Whoo hoo!*

"One more shot, Josh. Go for it."

If Josh could sink it, he might have the best score on this test. He closed his eyes to visualize, just as he had done in the motivational seminar. Okay, this was his drill. He saw himself putting the puck in the net. He opened his eyes and looked down at the puck. Then he looked at the hole. He took a deep breath and fired the puck as hard as he could.

When it hit the hole, it sank right through to the other side.

"*All right!*" Josh punched the air with his fist.

Peter gave him a high-five. "Tonight our line is

definitely getting a hat trick."

That night, NHL Selects won 8–4. Josh didn't quite score his hat trick. But he put in two goals. He also picked up an assist on a goal Peter scored and another on a goal Troy scored. Josh's line played the best by far, and Josh really felt as if he had helped them win the game.

Afterward, Gerald was waiting for everyone. "Post-game pizza in the cafeteria!"

Team Mexico was already in the cafeteria when Josh and his teammates arrived and, as soon as they saw Troy, they pointed and started speaking loudly in Spanish. One of them looked as if he was going to make a run at Troy, but his teammates grabbed him and held him back.

"What's with the Mexicans? Why are they so fired up?" Barry frowned at Troy. "They look peeved at you."

"It's nothing," said Troy. "They're just sore losers." He walked over to the pizza boxes. Josh followed right behind him.

Troy picked up a paper plate, napkin, and a couple slices of pizza. Josh stared at him with his eyebrows squished together. They had played the Mexicans in the first game *last week*. There was no way they were still peeved from that hockey game. This card business had gone on long enough. Troy had showed up ready to play that night, but Josh wasn't going to let him off the hook just because he played one good game. He didn't want to let Troy ruin the rest of his week at camp. Josh was ready to blast Troy. "I thought you were playing cards with the Swiss guys last night," Josh muttered to Troy so no one else could hear. He yanked a paper plate off the pile and grabbed a few pieces of pizza.

As they walked away from the table, Troy took a big bite of his pizza before he answered Josh. "Nah. Their counsellor wouldn't let them stay up because they had the early ice time this morning. I played with the guys from Team Mexico instead." He laughed. "I beat them bad." Then he wiped his mouth.

Josh shook his head. "That's obvious." Josh glanced over at the Mexican players before turning back to Troy. "I thought they didn't speak much English."

"They speak enough. Anyway, I took Spanish last year, so I know a few words. I don't think they play cards at home though. They sucked, and I won a load from them." He picked up his second piece of pizza and the cheese and pepperoni slid off onto his plate.

"You know you're not supposed to gamble at this camp. Someone is going to find out. You're being stupid," Josh said.

"It's okay. No one knows."

"It's not okay! You could get kicked out. We could lose because of you."

"Okay, okay, whatever. I'll stop." Troy flopped the toppings back on his pizza and scarfed down the entire piece.

Turmoil rumbled in Josh's stomach. He didn't believe Troy. Troy had lied all week. He was hurting the team. But Josh didn't know what to do. He didn't want to rat Troy out.

"You're sure you'll stop? You promise?"

"Hey," Troy patted Josh on the back. "I'm here to win too, you know."

"You better not be lying." Josh walked away from Troy.

13 Middle of the Night

"Psst, Josh."

Josh rolled over to see the whites of Sam's eyes in the dark. Sam was hovering above him.

Snores bounced off the walls. They sounded like guns going off in a James Bond movie. Josh glanced at Gerald, who was lying on his back with his mouth wide open, snoring violently.

"Troy is gone," whispered Sam.

"You're kidding, right?"

"He's up to something. Come on."

Josh slithered out of bed, trying to move silently, and followed Sam. Where was Troy now? When Josh had confronted him about gambling, Troy had promised Josh he wouldn't play cards anymore.

Josh and Sam tiptoed to the door. In the hallway, Sam stopped Josh with his hand. "Listen."

Josh heard the voices. "Who is that?" he whispered.

Sam shrugged. "Let's go find out."

They padded down the hall in bare feet, moving in the direction of the voices. As they got closer to the door, they could make out the words, "I raise you." It was Troy.

Josh clenched his fists. "He lied to me. They're playing cards," he whispered. "I wonder who he suckered in this time."

"Shh!" Sam whispered. "I want to hear this."

"But I don't have any money left." The voice replying to Troy had a Swiss accent. "He's with the Swiss guys ... " Josh whispered back.

"Guess I win then," said Troy.

Josh shook his head. The idiot actually thought winning money made him better than they were.

"But that's all my money for the rest of the week," said a Swiss player.

"Yeah, but you lost. That's the way it goes."

"I want my money back."

"No way! You lost."

"Give him his money back." It was another accented voice. "We've never played this game before. We didn't know the rules."

"You did too. Just borrow off one of your other teammates."

"I'll give you my stick instead."

"I don't want your stick. I play for money."

"We'll tell the counsellors you stole our money."

"Yeah, and I'll say you gambled with me, and then

we'll all be in trouble."

Josh's stomach churned. There was no way he could just stand back and let this happen. He straightened his back and stood tall. "Sam, I'm going in there. I have to tell Troy to give them back their money. He can't keep doing this." But for some reason, Josh couldn't move.

"I'm going to bed," they heard Troy say. Josh could hear the sound of Troy putting the cards and chips away. Then Troy's laughter. "If you want your money back, you could always lose to us in the game. Then I'll give it back."

"What do you mean? Lose our game on purpose?" The Swiss player sounded confused and angry. "We would never do that."

"I can't believe he would say that!" said Josh. His shock seemed to get his feet working. Josh and Sam stormed into the room.

Troy's eyes widened. "What are you guys doing up?"

"You're such a liar, Troy!" said Josh. "You told me you'd stop. You know there's a no gambling rule. Give them back their money."

"Why? I won it fair and square."

Josh shook his head. "Give it back. It's not like you need it."

"We played. I won."

"How could you ask them to throw a game?"

Josh's voice was loud and angry.

"It gets us into the championship."

"No one wants to get into a championship game like that," retorted Josh. "We're good enough to get in on our own."

"Guys, what's going on in here?" The voice came from the door of the room.

Josh spun around. His body tensed when he saw the steely look in Gerald's eyes.

"I asked what's going on."

"We're just playing cards," said Troy.

"In the middle of the night? Are you betting real money?"

"No."

Gerald looked directly at Josh. "Were you involved in this game?"

Josh angrily shook his head. He wasn't going to get in trouble when he didn't do anything. "No," he said firmly. "Sam and I woke up and heard some noises, so we came to find out where they were coming from."

"Were these guys betting?" Gerald was still directing his questions at Josh.

Gerald had helped Josh all week, encouraging and supporting him, and Troy had been a jerk. Josh didn't think he should have to be responsible for any of this, and there was no reason for Sam, or anyone else on the team, to be in trouble either. Josh looked from Gerald to Troy. Then he stared Troy in the eyes. "Troy, why don't you answer the question for me? After all, you're better than me at everything."

Josh looked back to Gerald. "I'm sorry, Gerald, this really has nothing to do with me. I wasn't involved. Sam wasn't involved either."

Gerald nodded, then gestured with his head for Josh and Sam to leave.

As they slipped out of the room, Sam said, "Thanks, Wattie."

14 Payback

Josh tossed and turned all night. Finally, when the sun was starting to come up, he fell into a fitful sleep. He must have slept for about an hour before he was woken by someone shaking him. "Josh," said Sam. "Get up."

Josh sat up, rubbing his eyes. He and Sam were the last ones left in the dorm room. "Where's Gerald?"

"Talking with the Swiss counsellor."

"Where's Troy?"

Sam shrugged. "Washroom, maybe."

"I have to talk to him."

Josh found Troy brushing his teeth. No one else was in the washroom. "Hey, Troy," he said.

"Hey." Troy wouldn't make eye contact with Josh, not even in the mirror.

"What happened last night?"

"I told Gerald the truth."

"I don't believe you."

"Well, I did, okay?"

"And?"

"I have to go home."

Josh looked down at the sink. "That bites." Josh remembered Troy saying that he hoped Josh wouldn't have to go home because of his diabetes. Now, Troy was the one going home, but for a very different reason.

"They're phoning my parents and telling them to arrange a flight for me. My dad is going to kill me."

Josh looked up and stared Troy in the eyes. "Why did you even start playing for money then when you knew it was against the rules? I told you to stop."

"Josh," Troy said, exasperation in his voice, "you don't get it. You have to get a leg up on the competition, and keep it there. That's the only way you'll get respect. It's the only way to win."

"No, it's not the only way to win. Look where cheating and breaking the rules got you: nowhere. And it's not the way to win friends, that's for sure. You know, on the ice, we *can* win against the Swiss team — the right way," said Josh.

Neither Josh nor Troy said anything for a few seconds. Finally, Troy broke the silence and said, "Does everyone know?"

"I'm not sure."

"They'll be cranked at me."

"Probably. But they'll get over it if we win."

"You guys will do fine." Troy paused. "You didn't

tell them that I asked the Swiss guys to throw the game, did you?"

"No. And I won't." Josh paused and squinted at Troy. "You didn't ask any of the other teams to throw any games, did you?"

"No." Troy jokingly raised his eyebrows. "I beat them fair and square."

"Is that supposed to be a joke?"

"Sorry."

Troy's shoulder slumped. "Sorry." He half-heartedly held up his knuckles. "Thanks, Josh. I guess I did get caught up in winning at the wrong thing."

Josh kept his hand at his side. He didn't want to get sucked in by Troy again. But when he saw a tear escape Troy's eye, Josh slowly lifted his hand and gave a half-hearted knuckle-punch back. "You were winning at hockey too."

"I know. Now you have to do it for both of us." Troy quickly swiped at his eyes and hung his head.

Josh patted him on the back.

Troy asked, "Are you still going to come to Winnipeg at the end of the summer?"

"And miss kicking your butt at wakeboarding?"

"Yeah, right." Troy's mouth curled into a small smile. "You might be kicking my butt at hockey, but you'll never catch me at wakeboarding."

Had Troy really just said something good about Josh's hockey? "Yeah, I'll catch you at the end of the summer. You think Uncle Brian will have cooled off by then?"

Troy grimaced. "Not likely. He'll ground me for sure. I'll probably have to work in his office doing boring stuff."

"You deserve it."

"Yeah, maybe." Troy paused. "Tell the guys good luck for me, okay?"

"I will."

★ ★ ★

"This won't be a real test," said Barry in the dressing room. "The two best players on the Swiss team aren't playing tonight. Troy is a loser for getting himself and them kicked out of the tournament."

Peter stood up. "Let's forget about what went down and just play hockey."

Josh was thankful that Peter understood how personally Josh was taking the situation. Everyone was talking about Troy being sent home. Troy was Josh's cousin, and Josh was the one who had invited him to the camp.

Barry smiled. "You're right, Arctic-boy. Let's just play hockey."

Even with the Swiss team missing its best players, the game started off like it was a horse race. Fast and skilled, the Swiss moved like lightning. They weren't huge hitters, but they knew how to carry the puck while skating at full speed.

Coach Manny had done some shuffling to fill Troy's spot on the line with Josh and Peter. Now they were on with Tony. Josh was happy with the choice — even though Tony wasn't as big and strong as Troy, he was a player who gave 110 percent.

Josh waited for his turn to go out. When he saw Barry wheeling over, Josh moved to the gate. Panting, Barry banged his stick and Gerald opened the door.

"Go, Josh," said Gerald.

Josh sped toward the play. A Swiss forward was heading down the ice, and Josh knew he needed to stop him along the boards. Josh flew in and braced his shoulder to hit him, but his opponent scooted right by. Josh slammed into the boards and crashed to the ground. He immediately picked himself up, shook off the stars dancing in his field of vision, and headed toward his own end zone. By now the Swiss player was heading directly at Sam. Sam was in his crouch. The Swiss player decked and roofed the puck. Sam stuck out his glove. The puck hit a small corner of the glove and bounced over the net. A lucky break!

Cameron, on defence for the NHL Selects, was behind the net, but so was the player who had just made the shot, and he was fore-checking like crazy.

Cameron rimmed the puck along the boards, but it was picked up by a Swiss defence on the blue line and kept in. He passed to his winger, who passed to his centre. Sam shuffled back and forth across the net as the Swiss cycled the puck. Peter swatted, trying to get an interception. Josh had to do something.

Suddenly, Peter's swatting paid off and he managed to push the puck out past the blue line. He exploded toward the puck. Josh followed, knowing if Peter went, he had to go too. He had to drive to the net.

Josh skated down the ice as hard as he could. The Swiss players caught up with him in no time, skating beside him.

End to end Peter skated with the puck, firing off a shot when he hit the hash marks. The Swiss goalie made the save, so Josh's line headed in for a change. On the bench, Josh gasped for air. His chest was pounding, his heart rate at its max.

"They're fast," said Tony, puffing. "I can't keep up."

"Sure you can," said Peter. "We can win this game. We need to stay in position and not run around chasing the puck. They'll beat us to the puck that way."

Barry, Carl, and Kevin were out. The play went up and down the ice. Neither team got away a shot.

"Keep skating," called Coach Manny from the bench. He turned to Josh. "We can hold them back by playing some good Canadian hitting hockey. We can beat their European speed with our brawn."

The game remained scoreless after the first period.

The intensity carried over into the second period.

After every shift, Josh was completely winded and his legs ached. The play went from one end to the other end and back again, and both teams skated full out.

Barry, Carl, and Kevin laid hit after hit. Peter hit hard. Josh hit too, time and again. To Josh's surprise, the constant hitting seemed to wear down the Swiss, and by the middle of the third period the NHL Selects were dominating the play. The score was still 0–0.

"Keep hitting and shooting," yelled Coach Manny. "You keep this up and you'll put one in."

Josh blasted on the ice with Coach Manny's words in his head. *Keep shooting!*

Peter had the puck on his stick and was flying down the ice. Josh chomped hard on his mouth guard and skated to follow him. If he drove to the net, he might be able to pick up a rebound. Peter saw Josh skating with him and, once over the blue line, he drop-passed the puck. Josh and Peter had been using this play throughout the two weeks and it seemed to work. Josh one-timed the puck, but his shot wasn't hard enough. The puck made it just to the net. Peter charged forward, lunging to get his stick on the puck. He tapped it and slid toward the goalpost. The puck skidded. The goalie reached. The puck landed behind the goalie!

Josh saw the ref make the motion for a goal.

The Swiss goalie rushed out of his net, headed toward the ref.

"Ref, the net was off." He pointed to the net.

Josh knew it wasn't. He knew the puck was in.

"The goal is in," the ref said, repeating his call.

Josh raced over to Peter and pulled him up to his feet. "Awesome goal!"

The score at the end of the game was 1–0 for the Selects.

★ ★ ★

At the post-game meal in the cafeteria, Josh wolfed down three pieces of pizza. Peter only ate one.

"What's wrong with you?" Josh joked.

"I didn't think I'd ever say this, but I'm sick of pizza," said Peter. "My stomach can't hold another piece."

The last evening at camp sped by, and lights-out came too quickly. Josh lay on his back and stared at the ceiling. He hadn't realized how tired he was. The previous night he hadn't slept well because of Troy. He yawned. The sound of everyone breathing made his eyes feel heavy. What had sounded the first night like a bad band warming up almost had rhythm after two weeks of camp.

15 Shootout

The classroom looked empty, with all the cots stripped and piled in a corner and all the bags packed and put in a heap off to the side. Josh had tied up his sleeping bag and crammed his suitcase with his dirty clothes.

For Josh, the two weeks had gone by fast. His parents and little sister Amy were coming to watch the final game and pick him up. The plan had been for Troy to get a ride with them to Calgary, but that obviously wasn't happening.

There wasn't much for the team to do during the day while they waited to get ready for the gold-medal game. They played soccer, but only until the sun got too hot.

"Let's take a break," said Peter. "Why don't we have a team meeting under that tree?" He pointed to a shady spot by the swing set.

"We're all here except Kevin. Where is he?" asked Josh.

"Loverboy is in the cafeteria," said Carl. "We can't wait around for him to finish talking to Nat-a-lie."

The NHL Selects gathered under the tree and the "team meeting" turned to talk of the future. Barry and Carl wanted to make Midget AAA, but knew they'd probably have to settle for AA. Peter was trying for Midget AAA as well, and everyone thought he'd make it. Josh knew that he would be lucky to make Midget A in Calgary.

In the midst of the hockey talk, Sam stood up. "Hey, look over there, guys. It's Loverboy with Natalie."

"Hey, he's holding her hand!" Josh pointed.

"Man, he is," said Barry.

Sam cupped his hands and yelled, "Hey, Loverboy!"

Kevin ignored them completely.

Josh and Sam rolled their eyes. "Geez, why did we write that poem again? I'm not sure who's worse when it comes to girls," whispered Josh. "We should have thought that one through before executing."

"Talk about back-firing in our faces," replied Sam.

★ ★ ★

The mood in the dressing room was sombre. Josh's stomach was tied up in knots. But the NHL Selects had won the day before. They could beat Team Switzerland again.

From the moment the puck dropped, Josh knew the game pace was going to be even faster than the last one. The Swiss team had rockets on their skates and were out for blood. Josh skated and skated.

Zack would be in net for the first half of the game and Sam was in net of the second half. The first goal was scored by the Swiss. Zack went down too early and the puck was lobbed over his right shoulder. The whistle blew, and Josh's line was out. Josh skated over to Zack and gently tapped his stick on the goalie's pads. "It's okay," he said. "We'll get it back."

As soon as the puck dropped, Tony battled for it at centre ice. Peter moved in for support and ended up with the puck on his stick. Josh knew he had to get going into the Swiss zone. Peter bounced the puck off the boards. Tony swung in and picked it up. Josh pushed over the blue line and headed straight for the net. Tony was on fire, rushing down the far side, keeping one stride ahead of the Swiss player. He looked up, saw Josh, and fired a pass to him. Josh picked it up and was going to take a shot when he saw Tony racing to the open side of the net. Peter was banging guys around, tying them up. Josh batted the puck to Tony, who drilled it. The puck flew past the goalie.

Josh ran on his skates. *Yes!* Tony had scored his first tournament goal.

"Great goal," said Josh.

"Thanks for the pass." Tony beamed. "We're moving."

Neither team scored again in the first period, so the score remained tied 1–1. By the middle of the second period, the score was still tied at 2–2. Barry had put an amazing goal in the net on a slapshot from the hash marks. Then a Swiss player had scored a goal using the spinnerama move that Josh had practiced, but by shooting the puck on his backhand instead of his forehand.

Coach Manny called Zack off at the game's halfway mark. Skating with confidence, Sam went to his net. He batted both posts with his big goalie stick, and got in his crouch.

Sam didn't let one goal in, making some unbelievable saves. But the Swiss goalie played just as well.

The game ended in a 2–2 tie.

Coach Manny gathered the NHL Selects at the bench. "Okay, guys. We're into a shootout situation."

Josh had never been selected for a shootout. If only Coach Manny would call his name. He knew he could do this; he wanted the chance. His stomach flip-flopped. Coach Manny and Gerald conferred, and Josh sucked in a deep breath when he saw Gerald look his way.

"Listen up," said Coach Manny. "Here's my list, based on performance over the last two weeks. Barry, Carl, Peter, Kevin, and … Josh. Sam, you'll stay in net."

Josh felt his stomach lurch. His hands sweated under his gloves. His face prickled with heat. Now that he had the opportunity to prove himself in the shootout, he wanted to throw up.

The Swiss went first, and Sam made a spectacular glove save. The NHL Selects bench erupted in cheers.

Next, Barry lined up at centre ice. Josh watched, holding his breath. Barry took long strides and went to the outside. The Swiss goalie shuffled over and tried to poke-check the puck from Barry, but Barry toed the puck and flipped it in the open side of the net. Josh raised his arms and cheered. They were up 1–0 in the shootout.

The next Swiss player sunk one past Sam in an amazing deke. Sam skated out of his net for a little breather.

Then Carl went, and missed. When the next Swiss player failed to make the shot, sweat rolled down Josh's face. He might actually have to take the shot.

As Peter was lining up at centre ice, Josh tried to breathe deeply to get the pains out of his stomach.

Suddenly, around Josh the bench went crazy. Peter had just scored! The NHL Selects were up 2–1. With Peter's goal going in there was a chance that Josh wouldn't have to take his penalty shot.

Josh watched closely as the next Swiss shooter came down the ice. He tried to take a slapshot from too far out. Sam easily made the save.

I can't do a slapshot from far out, thought Josh.

Fourth in line for the NHL Selects was Kevin. "Come on, Loverboy," whispered Josh.

Kevin took off with tremendous speed. He raced toward the net and, in a smooth move, backhanded the puck. Somehow the Swiss goalie hit it with his blocker and the puck bounced out front.

If the Swiss put the next one in, then the shootout score would be even and Josh would have to take a shot. If the Swiss shooter missed, the Selects would win without Josh shooting.

Josh lowered his head and stared at his gloves. His knees felt as if they might buckle. When he heard the loud cheer coming from the Swiss bench, he knew the score was 2–2. Josh was the only shooter left.

"You're out, Josh." Coach Manny's voice sounded faint through the sound of the blood rushing in Josh's ears.

"Go, Josh," said Barry.

"You can do it, Josh," said Carl.

Peter tapped Josh on the shoulder. "Remember. Pick your spot, hold it in your mind for accuracy, then get that rapid release."

Josh stepped on the ice. He lined up at centre ice. He blew out a rush of air and stared at the goalie. Where would he shoot? His back-hand wasn't strong. There was no way he could try the spinnerama move yet. What about the five-hole? He visualized where he would put the puck. At the skills centre he'd been able to put the puck in the net. He could do the same thing now. The whistle blew.

Josh knew he didn't need to do anything fancy. All he needed to do was make a low, hard shot.

He skated toward the goalie, stick-handling the puck, and picking up speed. When he was close enough, he eyed the goalie, picked his spot, held it in his mind, then rifled the puck as hard as he could.

It zoomed toward the goalie's five-hole. The goalie lowered into his butterfly. But the puck kept zooming, right through the five-hole.

When it hit the back of the net, Josh's team jumped the boards, skating like crazy toward him. They all threw their gloves in the air. Within seconds, the ice was covered with gloves and sticks. Sam whipped his blocker and catcher in the air and raced to Josh. He was first to hug him.

Peter was next, and he jumped so high that Josh almost fell over. "You did it!"

"We are the champions!" Barry jumped on Peter's back. With the extra weight, Josh toppled to the ice. He held his hands over his head as his whole team dog-piled him. Underneath the bodies of old friends and new friends, Josh grinned.

All he could think of was one thing. Hockey is the greatest sport in the world.

Other books you'll enjoy in the Sports Stories series

Ice Hockey

❑ *Cross-Check* by Lorna Schultz Nicholson
Josh, Peter, and Sam are thrilled to be reunited at a hockey tournament in Kelowna, but a lot has changed. All three boys now play on different teams. Can they remain friends as they all compete to be in the gold medal game?

❑ *The Enforcer* by Bill Swan
When Jack's hockey coach moves, Jack's hockey-crazy grandfather P.J. steps into the role. But can the team adapt to Grandpa P.J.'s old-school methods?

❑ *Power Play* by Michele Martin Bossley
An early-season injury causes Zach Thomas to play timidly, and a school bully just makes matters worse. Will a famous hockey player be able to help Zach sort things out?

❑ *Danger Zone* by Michele Martin Bossley
When Jason accidentally checks a player from behind, the boy is seriously hurt. Jason is devastated when the boy's parents want him suspended from the league.

❑ *A Goal in Sight* by Jacqueline Guest
When Aiden has to perform one hundred hours of community service, he is assigned to help a blind hockey player whose team is Calgary's Seeing Ice Dogs.

❑ *Ice Attack* by Beatrice Vandervelde
Alex and Bill used to be an unbeatable combination on the Lakers hockey team. Now that they are enemies, Alex is thinking about quitting.

❑ *Red-Line Blues* by Camilla Reghelini Rivers
Lee's hockey coach is only interested in the hotshots on his team. Ordinary players like him spend their time warming the bench.

❑ *Goon Squad* by Michele Martin Bossley
Jason knows he shouldn't play dirty, but the coach of his hockey team is telling him otherwise. This book is the exciting follow-up to *Power Play* and *Danger Zone*.

❑ *Interference* by Lorna Schultz Nicholson
Josh has finally made it to an elite hockey team, but his undiagnosed type one diabetes is working against him — and getting more serious by the day.

❑ *Deflection! by Bill Swan*
Jake and his two best friends play road hockey together and are members of the same league team. But some personal rivalries and interference from Jake's three all-too-supportive grandfathers start to create tension among the players.

❑ *Misconduct* by Beverly Scudamore
Matthew has always been a popular student and hockey player. But after an altercation with a tough kid named Dillon at hockey camp, Matt finds himself number one on the bully's hit list.

❑ *Roughing by Lorna Schultz Nicholson*
Josh is off to an elite hockey camp for the summer, where his roommate, Peter, is skilled enough to give Kevin, the star junior player, some serious competition, creating trouble on and off the ice.

❑ *Home Ice* by Beatrice Vandervelde
Leigh Aberdeen is determined to win the hockey championship with a new, all girls team, the Chinooks.

❑ *Against the Boards* by Lorna Schultz Nicholson
Peter has made it onto an AAA Bantam team and is now playing hockey in Edmonton. But this shy boy from the Northwest Territories is having a hard time adjusting to his new life.

❑ *Delaying the Game* by Lorna Schultz Nicholson
When Shane comes along, Kaleigh finds herself unsure whether she can balance hockey, her friendships, and this new dating-life.

❑ *Two on One* by C.A. Forsyth
When Jeff's hockey team gets a new coach, his sister Melody starts to get more attention as the team's shining talent.

❑ *Icebreaker* by Steven Barwin
Gregg Stokes can tell you exactly when his life took a turn for the worse. It was the day his new stepsister, Amy, joined the starting line-up of his hockey team.

❑ *Too Many Men* by Lorna Schultz Nicholson
Sam has just moved with his family to Ottawa. He's quickly made first goalie on the Kanata Kings, but he feels insecure about his place on the team and at school

Golf

❑ *Drive* by Eric Howling
Jake gets the once-in-a-lifetime opportunity to be taught by a golf pro, but if he wants to take his game to the next level, he'll have to stand up to his bullies, the Fearsome Foursome.

Skateboarding

❑ *SK8TER* by Lorna Schultz Nicholson
Talented Alisha might be able to coach Jordy to win the skateboarding competition, but what will his friends think about Jordy getting advice from a cute girl?

Soccer

❑ *Falling Star* by Robert Rayner
Edison Flood is losing his nerve. Can Edison's new teammates help him rediscover his love of soccer, or has his star fallen for good?